To

FEMI,

MANY THANKS FOR YOUR SUPPORT.
MAY THE LORD GOD TRULY BLESS THE
FAMILY & YOU.

YOU ARE A TRUE BROTHER & A FRIEND.

STAY BLESSED

19/05/2018

Adéwálé John Adéyeyè was born in Marina, Lagos, Nigeria and studied in England. In 2005, he qualified as an Architect and gained a Master's degree in the subject in 2007. He began writing this novel, his first, whilst completing his MArch thesis. Originally attracted by the imaginative freedom literature offers, he soon discovered that the discipline required for writing an academic paper is also applicable to writing a novel.

Imagination n

1 the faculty or action producing ideas, esp. mental images of what is not present or has been experienced. 2 mental creative ability. 3 the ability to deal resourcefully with unexpected or unusual problems, circumstances, etc. 4 ... a creative act of perception that joins passive and active elements in thinking and imposes unity on the poetic material.

Collins English Dictionary, Fourth Edition, 1998, p771.

ADÉWÁLÉ ADÉYẸYÈ

Jelë

LIQUID WORDS PUBLISHING

978-0-9565346-0-6

A CIP catalogue record for this book
is available from the British Library.

ISBN 978-0- 9565346-0-6

An imprint of
Liquid Words Publishing Ltd.

www.adewaleadeyeyeauthor.com

To my darling Wife Mary - my only.

To Adeonai - my first.

To Carl, and Kathy - my enablers.

To my Family - my anchor.

To Imagination - my ally.

To Almighty God - my Creator.

Jelë

Chapter One

VOICE

Remember the King and the Queen,
And their throne that faces the West,
Much trouble brews in their chests,
Calamity is spread on their skin.

The love,
The strong love will soon be broken,
And tears will fill all.

Where are their mighty men of battle?
Where is their beautiful Princess?
Surely one can save,
Surely all have the strength.

The Queen,
Her bejeweled neckwear will be loosed,
Her precious stone buried.

The King,
His crown of glory will be taken,
His ruling staff broken,
Naked, he shall flee.

Remember the Prince and the Princess,
He with the watery eyes,
She with her green eyes and treasured pearls.

Remember the King and the Queen,
Remember, remember. . .

Mother, mother. 'Is that you?' Mother. . .

Chapter Two

STRONGER

This must be the end, I whispered with a fading breath. To learn the things I do not know, and then forget those I have learned seemed the biggest loss of all. To start afresh is always a daunting task. Tell me what you know is a tougher question than to explain what one does not know, because in not knowing, all rules are abandoned, and no expectations are unfulfilled. Losing someone or something is applicable to us all. Is it not in defeat that champions arise?

Some believe it makes individuals stronger.

Why then is there strength in despair?

Why are precious stones buried in the muddy waters of hardship?

Why does power befriend sorrow and the bottomless

pit harbour renewed spirit?

Losing then is not the end. It cannot be, rather it is the beginning of a rekindled spirit. Surely it is better to have had and then lost, than to have not had at all; to have danced in the rain and feel its warm trickles, than to have not tasted this great fruit called life.

Confusion has engrafted itself unto me, as I wonder aimlessly within these invisible walls. Surely, it is better to grow than to shrivel, and die, better I know, to progress than to regress.

As I lay here, these and many other thoughts stomp through my mind. The answers whether welcomed or not rip the very gut from within me. For now, what was once wrong has become right, and what was right is now abhorrent. I now realise that when someone is alive, they can actually be dead, and when the gift of breath has escaped them, they could be reveling in the land of the living. Everything it seems has fled from me.

I have been traveling for a while now, and hunger is the only lullaby that rocks me to sleep. At times, it treats me like a bully that just cannot get enough. It had gripped me like a woman giving birth at an early age, it's claws of pang grips me as if it needs my life for its.

Thirst too showed no mercy. It dragged me in the dry desert like an underpaid executioner; my cries only spurned it on. Tiredness too clamours me like wet clothes in a monsoon.

'Do I really need these legs of mine?' I wondered. Self-amputation will surely lighten the load, but then I will leave a trail of blood, and beasts will hound me. The grainy sea and the water from the blue sea will soon put a stop to that.

'That is it', I said to myself.

Whatever I come across first is the choice to make - flint, death, or a helper.

Well, the flint has to be large enough to dig in between my groin and thigh, pull the skin to one side, and dig into the groove.

'Do I cut from front to back or back to front?'

'What of the pain?'

'What pain?' I asked myself.

This is no time for indecision. I now know the intricate creases of its smile, and the agony it expels with its foul breath. That aside for now.

'What if the flint brakes?'

Then I will have a flint in the groin.

'What if the helper arrives at that very moment and wit-nesses my indulgence in self-torture, will they not just flee?'

It does not really matter, who cares how I get there, as long as I am there.

'What am I saying?

Why does my mind run away like the waterfall?'

My tongue too ignored my wishes to speak; it had be-come a close relative with the attic of my mouth. They both make jest at me, adamant that we are sworn enemies.

When I look to the left, my eyes move to the right. When I try to throw a quick glance to the right, my eyeballs reluctantly sliver to the left. My tools for seeing have become both an amusement, and weapons of torture in my skull. They both dance eloquently and independently to a tune of a rusty merry-go-round.

My legs, escaping butchering for now, are heavy under

me. Each step had become a chore, and each advance takes the very life I am trying to preserve.

'Shall I stop?'

My limbs questioned this not but I dare ask my brain for help, the thoughts will only rattle around in the echoing chamber, and then spit in my face for disturbing its slumber.

I must go on. I must crawl towards my invisible destination with an unknown distance. Now, and then I see my destination only a few strides away from me, but it evaporates every time I get close.

'Oh, it is no use' I mumbled.

Many have gone before me surely much more will follow.

Chapter Three

BEASTS IN ME

The night still haunts me. The screams, the cries, and the panic in the settlement; tears bathed me as I witnessed the fall of my people. All that I have now is the haunting memories of both young and old. Things I had are now lost, those I knew are now nothing but fading recollections.

There is no power in sorrow but torment; neither is there an ally in the thicket of despair. I am a living proof of that. I have journeyed to and through still confusion is all that befriended me. Yet, this life still burns in me, 'Why does it not just flicker, fade, and end?'

My sight has become a blurry vision of reality, night light comes and goes, but they register not with me. My days are full of grief and when I lay my eyes in the darkness of rest, all I see are The Beasts of the Night devouring my people.

The night is when they are ever present, preferring the cloak of darkness. Their skin and furs coloured with a mixture of the colours of the night, and the grainy sea. They glide gently towards their prey that always realise their intensions at the wrong side of the gate of death. When they hunt alone, they are deadly; when they hunt in packs, undeterrable. Their head is triple-skulled, and they have eyes that glow like the high light. Their mouth is armed with deadly teeth, and sharp claws decorate their arms and legs. The Beasts of the Night seem to be more than just predators; they take prey for food as if it was pre-ordained.

When they are on a hunt from the settlement, it becomes a deadly game of the hunter been hunted by the Dynasty of the North. Over time, they developed methods of taking down the ferocious beasts. Their most effective are the ring of arrows. Here, each hunter has a given target on the Beasts with its sequence, more importantly, the order in which it should enter The Beast's neck. Each positioned to inflict the most harm, death delivered in sharp and heavy doses. These were hunters of the wild with incredible hand speed whether left or right; be it with spears or arrows.

For centuries, The Beasts of the Night had often struck and killed. Knowing this, the Dynasty has spread glowing dye around the bushes of the settlement where they launch their attacks. Their speed is so fast that that look like streams of fire and light. The scattering, galloping heads of brightness spread like a swarm of bees when they run. This signals only one thing to the Dynasty: Danger. Nonetheless, it has always been a losing battle for The Beasts, but this season, things were going to be different.

At their emergence that frightful night, the huntsmen based on top of the trees and mountains quickly rushed down. The settlement in front of them were been attacked by what seemed to be an invisible force. From a distance, people, crops, and live stocks seem to disappear in a cloud of the grainy sea. To their rear, The Beasts chasing with lightening speed.

We all panicked, and confusion was our only destination. The men for the first time were at a loss as to what was happening, The Beasts attacked from above and seemingly below the ground. The ferociousness and the number of The Beasts was one never before witnessed.

What followed was a frenzy of killing. Spears and arrows

rained, panic gripped all as fire swept through the lush paradise. The event, called the Tiron-tamada was the first time the Dynasties felt that the Creator never helped them, frustrated that a vision was not shown to them. That day, all that I believed; I questioned. All we had disappeared.

The attack seemed pre-planned and the Beasts had a determination of death etched onto their faces. This, the Beasts felt was their time, time for revenge. They wiped out all my people, the crops, and our possessions.

I survived only after a blow to the head by the powerful jaw of my people's fate. Crawling on all fours, a sudden shiver embraced me tight like a long lost friend. I saw anger reach out to grab me from the eyes of the triple-skulled grim reaper. I shivered and fell down a crevice where I became wedged between the rock faces. Its saliva generously bathed my head as it frantically ran around, and tried to prise me out. I smelt annoyance in its breath as it paced back and forth. It roared, angry that one got away.

Terrified by the ordeal and after days in its grip, the crevice released me. Whether it was my pungent body odour, its loss of interest in human flesh or that I was now slim enough to pass through the eye of a needle, my mind was not coherent enough to ask it or even thank it for that matter.

Now, lost in the wilderness, I found myself in a place I could only describe as nowhere. Its barrenness made me realise my loneliness and I remembered her . . .

There she is again,
My love,
Precious to me she was,
Like a delicate flower amidst thorns.

I said to her,
If you feel not the same,
Speak so,
I hope the chosen,
Adores you more than I am able.

If I am not the one,
Why does your name rapture in my heart?
If you are not for me,
Why do your thoughts leave me not?

But, if I am the one,

Then this day is sweeter than honey,

Greater than the high light in the day,

Better than even the cool, calming springs.

Oh beautiful girl,

Joy uncountable you brought to me,

Love, more than I imagined,

You move me,

Your loving lures me,

It heals me.

When I am with you,

All that I need is near,

When you are not here,

All is far.

When I look to the left,

I want to see your face,

When I look to the right,

I must see you.

You are closer to me than my breath,

I know you more than my face,

You dwell in my mind in the day,

And let go not of my dreams at nights.

Days tick on,

Nights fold into each another,

The high light reaches out,

The night light melts the shadow,

Beautiful they are,

Magical they may be,

But without you to share them,

Empty are their works.

Oh Jelë,

I will say to the night light,

Why bother shine,

And to the high light of day,

Why bother smile.

As the cloud grows,

And is massaged by the high light,

As the star glides,

And are kissed by the night light,

So to I long for you,

Impossible it is not to.

Oh girl,

At night, I hold you,

But you disappear,

Like the mist at daybreak,

I converse with you,

And our words are forever sweet.

Surely, you are here,

My words fall,

But bear no fruit,

My tears run,

But leave no tracks.

Surely, you are here,

Your scent I smell, you I touch,

Not even death can separate us,

Its claws have no grip,

It's jaw, no bite.

When you are near,
Pain and despair are far.

If I became a skeleton,
And they bathe me in the blue sea water,
If they took me to the grinding stone,
And made me witness the powder from my fingers,
And I blow in the wind like ashes.

If the rain comes,
And I am washed,
Amongst the jagged edges of the rock,
And between the smooth pebbles faces.

If the wilder-beast in its thirst gulps me,
I will possess his body,
And come to look for you.

If when I am gone,
You see a wilder-beast startle,

Then stare at you,

Believe me,

It is not an ordinary beast.

If I roll down the river,

And tumble into the blue sea,

If I cannot hold back the torrents of the flood,

Like my memories of you,

If I slide to the bottom of the lake,

And pass the waving algae's,

And make my way down to the abyss,

I will still long for you.

I will wrestle the biggest beasts of the deep,

And brave the warm currents on my back,

I will possess him,

Beach him,

So that I can see you by the river's edge.

I will challenge even the Creator,

For a fight over you,

I will tell her to come down from upon high,

And not use the special powers hidden in her locket.

I will ask her to come and face me,

Once she rids herself of her hidden powers,

We will grip in a wrestle,

Telling her not to change into the wind,

Or flee like a bird.

Where should we battle?

Upon the mountain high of course,

I will strip myself bare,

And grit my teeth in anticipation.

I will clasp my hand,

And steady my foothold,

I will refuse to loose,

And not let fear grip me,

For I demanded this battle.

All that are around will see,

They will be witnesses,
And forever tell the story,
Of my deep love for you.

But all this is now nothing but a wish,
Fate took you before me,
Your destiny was swifter than I could run,
What I feel is more than jealousy,
As I drink from this bitter goblet called 'Now',
Consuming my blue sea of grief.

Does the Creator know not?
That all this is too much for me?

I sleep,
Hoping for it to be the last,
Anger grips me again,
As my deep black meets the colours of life,

I feel a stranger to joy,
As the day announces its arrival boldly,
I watch in bitterness,

As the colours of the rising high light,
Take off its dark outer garments

Again I wish,
Again I waited,
Again,
You are not here.

Chapter Four

THE MAD SEER

I was at the beginning of my gathering when lying there before me, I saw what I thought was a person . . .

'Stop right there. You are not going to kill this one as well are you?'

'Kill, but why?'

'Why, your memory indeed is short. You have forgotten, have you? The young girl at Kutu that you told to walk through the fire of life, that she will not get hurt - she was scarred for life - whilst you, as you proclaimed, was 'trying to cure her illness'. Forgotten have you? How very conven-

ient.'

'I am here to save this young man.'

'Ha ha ha, you are indeed a fool. Fear him that fears his own shadow; flee the imbecile that is afraid of the mist of his own breath, and mistakes it for a curse from his enemies. A fool indeed is he who confuses taking a life with giving it.'

'You must have me confused with a murderer that you were once an accomplice. Why do you take me for a rogue?'

'Shut up you charlatan. My eyes have seen many wonders but never have I seen a man hold out his palms, and says he does not know how to use them. You know me, since birth I have known you, day in day out, we commune . . .'

'Silence you buffoon. You go on and on yet you fail to impart knowledge, wisdom too escapes your drivel.'

'Me, buffoon? You surprise me.'

'Quite, you are nothing but a cloud that clears with the rising of the high light, nothing but darkness that scampers at the slight sniff of light. So you come again, back are you from the land of the damned?'

'Why do you tire not at your repeated failure? I have a new name for you, "Failure." You failed in the past, and you will meet the same end today.'

Me, Failure? How can you look at your own reflection on a clear day, and on the still waters, and wish what you see should perish? Maybe in your dim-wit, you will soon realise that unlike you, I drink not from the well of failure, and feast gluttonously not on its high table'. 'This way sir,' they say to you, as you are ushered to dine with the damned. I have witnessed it in my own presence.

Why do you wonder the land with no fixed abode?

Why are you caste out of all settlements?

'Why,' I ask, 'did the Rameta birds refused your plea to befriend them?

Did you think that I had forgotten your evil ways? It was indeed a wonderful day when the Dynasty slung you out of their midst? You may have forgotten, but it is clear in my. . .'

'Silence, my very core rejects you. Each time you speak, bitter vomit gurgles in my throat . . .'

'No I will not hold on to my words, you one-eyed-monster. Remember your last days with your people, as they stripped you naked, and set the wilder-beasts onto you. The gash to your head dislodged your eye, oh how sweet.'

'Ha-ha, ha-ha, your repulsive appearance brings joy to me, now that the beasts have mangled your face. No wonder your seed-sized memory pervades you.'

'You call day night, and night day, your mind merely mirrors your life. . . scattered and abhorrent. So now, you have found yourself another victim. You learn not, and reject advice like work in the eyes of a lazy man. I will not let your tainted hands touch this young man, for all that you do is wrong.'

'When are you going to let these people be?'

'This land wants you not.' You slaughter innocent wilder-beasts on your bloody altar of shame, and take them

not for meat but for their hide and intestines. You have cursed the rivers, and destroyed forests. You turned the once lush garden of the East to a barren land, and blinded the innocent girl, Jelë.'

'What good, I ask, have you done since your discharge from that cursed womb?'

'Any wonder then why blasphemies afflict you all day long. So, you are still practicing the same old rubbish. Burning your foul incense, and whispering gibberish to yourself.'

'Quick, Safari.'

'Behind you: a wilder-beast.'

'Chase it.'

'Rip its heart and liver out while it still beats.'

'Lay it on the virgin rock of Sube-mai.'

'Wrap it with the algae of Sandosa.'

'Rummage.'

'Quickly; in your Ball of Wonder.'

'Find it.'

'Find the other half of the claw of the Choord bird.'

'He, hee, the buffoon actually thought there was a wilder-beast near.'

'You disappoint me.'

'If you are so good, and your ways so righteous, why have you not found a cure for yourself?'
'Why I ask, are you neither a person nor a beast?'
'Is it because both have rejected you?'

'There are reasons why the high light climbs the waving blue sea, and then falls. Reasons exist for the great floods of the South. Reasons too for the violent volcanoes of Mount Sumbiti and many reasons indeed shroud the creation of people.'

'When we lack knowledge, all is confusing; when we breathe without wisdom; even paradise becomes an affliction to the soul. When we know not love, its sweet-est affections are but redundant acts and its joy like a potent scent with no fragrant.'

'You confused my handy-work with those that kill with no conscience and proclaim that all I do is wrong. You gather these ill thoughts in your mind and turn them into your warped reality to fulfill your abhorrent fantasy. Still, you surprise me not. Before you spoke, I knew the words you will utter, before you shaped your thoughts, your stench had engulfed me.'

'Why are your days never bright but damp and dark? Why do you speak not one good word of me?'

'You know why, you fake.'

'Instead, you polish your phrases of bitterness against me, do you not know that your words tamper not my foundation. The shackles you try to bind me with have no strength. You string poisonous sentences together like fine neckwear, but your words afflict me not.'

'You have forgotten that I it was, that entertained the services of the beasts to get you out of my head, out of my life. As its jaw, and sabre tooth plunge my flesh, and skull, my blood rolled slow, thick, and laboured as if afraid of the air; stunned in its path by my self-cruelty.'

'I hope you also enjoyed the sweet agonizing pain I endured and basked in the brief, sweet aroma of death. I pleaded for you not to receive the same help given by Sua, the woman from Ite that saved me from the warm grasp of death. The disfigurements that you are familiar with are a proof that you have no power over me.'

'Yes, the powder of my creation blinded the young

girl Jelë. In return for her kindness, Sua wanted a cure for her desperately ill twins.'

'Was it not you, Mystery, who cornered her, and poisoned her mind?'

'You indeed told her to add other strange ingredients to my potion. You it was, that changed Jelë's fate. Sua's daughter blew the powder into the face of that innocent child, her childhood friend. Her panic breathing and frantic rubbing of the eyes only dragged her further into the bottomless darkness.'

'Liar, whose imagination is running wild now, always finding excuses for your existence . . .'

'So Mystery, go I say, to the land where the inhabitants breathe not, and daylight pays them not a visit. Go I say, to where the dreaded beasts dwell. Crawl I urge you, into the path of the hot river; climb why don't you into the jaws of The Beasts of the night.'

The people were right, you are indeed a Mad Seer, on your best days a lunatic. Me, leave you alone? Never. Never, you hear me. Better, a fool to die as a man than a man to die a fool, the latter indeed shall be your lot.'

'Leave, and let me get on with saving this young man, time spent on you is but a waste, those spent on him, precious.'

'Lying there before me, I saw what I thought was a person. At first, I thought he was from the Dynasty of the North, a place where our people once possessed. His markings, although it was less clear, it was ones I have not seen before. What I saw, I could not ignore. For now, he looked not like a person, but more like a fallen tree, covered in powder earth.'

'How could this be,' I asked myself.

'How did he survive?'

'Where had he been?'

'Is he dead or just in deep sleep?'

'The anguish raged within me and I screamed with all my might, son of man, son of Creator, hear my voice, for you have journeyed for too long for you to give up now . . .'

'Oh no, not again . . .'

'I possessed on me not enough water to quench your thirst or berries to fill your hunger. . .'

'You are out of your poisonous offerings. What is a relief. . .'

'What I bring is greater than this. Arise, I screamed, and screamed again. Why do you lie there, and refuse to hear my call?'

'Why lay motionless like the mountain of Sube, and speak not with the breath gifted to you?'

'Why are you refusing to walk with your fellow people? . . .'

'Finally, you have lost your murdering touch . . .'

'We know your plight at the Tiron-tamada that you

have lost all your people, and your loved ones are no longer here. Oh, son of our Dynasty, we mourned for all the people, and beasts that resided in the land to the North.'

'Oh son, the one from the heritage of warriors. From the land of the blessed earth; the place of amazing splendour and beauty.'

'Oh, son of our people from the cradle of plenty, the delightful aromas, sensual perfumes, and oils, awake for this is not your lot.'

'I employ you to stand up and take back the breath that you have abandoned. For a whole day, and longer if needed I will continue to call upon you. I shall keep pleading with the Creator until you return to our midst until you are walking and uttering your voice.

'Oh young man, destined to carry his father's clan to the next generation, pay heed to my voice . . .'

'Ha, ha-ha, I think you need to shout louder. Plea harder; you confused buffoon.'

'The wind has no choice but to blow and the high

light questions not to shine, they dare not question the Maker. The birds in the high sea ask not how to fly, and as the cycle of life is ever new; I plea to the Creator to show mercy onto you.'

'As surely as all living things need water for their existence, as the beasts need the earth under their feet; and as night needs the day, I beg the Creator to return his breath back into you.'

'Once again I plea, do not only give life, give him life beyond his existence. Let there be many generations after him. Let uncountable children live through him; let men, and women descent from his heritage.'

'I continued in my utterance, although my body was weak . . .'

'Weakness indeed is that not what you consume like water day-after-day . . .'

'Then suddenly, a great quietness fell upon us. It rolled as if made from the finest virgin silk. The most beautiful quietness furnished the landscape. In front of us was quietness. At a distance, to the left, to the right, and as far as the eyes can see, all I saw was quietness, like a magnificent cloud pregnant with rain.'

'It flowed like the warm waves of the South, and the landscape seemed enchanted by the bliss silence. I saw the soul of quietness.'

'At that moment, the mighty noise had no power. It had no legs to climb the mighty rocks of mute. Then a cold wind blowing from the North to the South came.

'Suddenly, out of nowhere came thunder. The size and might that I have never witnessed before. Its colour was as clear as day with a myriad mix of the colours of the forest. I staggered and fell at the sight of it. I was disorientated by the sound of it as it shook me from within . . .'

'You have done it now Safarai, upsetting the Creator. Curse be onto you; curse be onto . . .'

'My face buried in the ground in awe. I was terrified to the point where my heart pondered to beat, but I knew something was happening although its intension pervaded me.'

'I peaked from the corner of my eye and watched as the air around us swirled with vengeance and anger. The force of the thunder shook me as if its anger was for my sole consumption.'

'Clouds, thick clouds, big clouds, bad clouds, small clouds, all embraced us. Then, I saw the thunder possessing his body, shaking him vigorously back and forth . . .'

'Murderer, murderer, murderer. . .'

'He twitched as if been awaken from a deep sleep. Then, rose up gauntly, his head, shoulder, and arm slumped by his side, his legs looking too weak to carry him, his eyes too dim to see.'
'Dust gathered, grainy sea reformed, branches, grass, powder earth, all began dancing around us. I tried to escape but the soil held me; I tried with all my might to break free but to no avail. Awe had replaced my bones, and terror instead of blood. The joy I once felt vanished like the Dynasty of the East in hibernation.'

'"Ground" I shouted, "open up and swallow me

whole", but my efforts were wasted.'

'My body was shaking in fear as if dancing like the Dynasty of the South. I entered into a spasm, my voice escaped me, my good eye turned blurry desperately trying to keep in view of what was happening to the young man.'

'Then, I saw him being raised into the air by the force of the thunder. His eyes were now like the colour of blood but he could not see. He turned towards me, his lips moved frantically, but he uttered no words I could hear. Then, I closed my eye, and felt an inner peace within me.'

'Liar, killer. Oh, revenge is so sweet. Now it is your turn to join those you fed the meal of death, life taker. Hope the gutter becomes your grave and your tombstone collapses on your gravediggers.

Hope your descendants dig up your bones, and sell it for dry-wood, and dump it into a fouled-waterlogged field, you evil clown.'

Chapter Five

SAFARAI

Flickering between life and unconsciousness; meandering between dreams and visions. Suddenly, out of nowhere, I saw what I thought was a beast. At first, I thought my long lost triple-skulled killer friend had finally caught up with me. The thing looked like a beast; it... must be a beast. However hard I tried, it was still difficult to make it out.

My mind and I were still battling with the rage of confusion. It seemed, we were entrapped in a sinister game of hide and seek. Occasionally, anger erupts in me, and I scream:

'Where have you been?'

It remained silent and slowly tightens its throbbing rope of pain around my head until I bled.

The thing moved unlike any other thing I have seen

and behaved not like any beast I had encountered. Now, fear
had escaped me only curiosity filled me like air.

The closer it got, the less I understood of it. It walked as if it
only had one leg and with no head. It was dressed as if shed-
ding its skin. Behind it dragged something wrapped-up in all
manner of leaves, twigs, and barks, this was then tied halfway
up its body. As it walked, the thing behind it swung from left
to right. The distant, settling powder-earth behind it echoed
its path.'

'What is in that thing?' and what is this thing?' I asked
myself.

It looked like a walking blown away leaf with a lethal
tail. Now and then, it mysteriously hops as if to fly like a bird,
and then rolled on the ground like a beast. As it moved closer,
I saw it more clearly, thanks to the welcomed return of my
senses - it indeed was a person, a man.

He drifted as he approached, even though the wind
was not strong enough to convince him of its movements. He
staggered as if hallucinating, often disappearing beyond my
peripheral. He went first to the left, then to the right, then
staggers to the left again.

He had grey, roughed, earth-filled hair, and dirt filled face. As he slowly emerged, he was coughing, chewing, and spitting things to the ground, some of them catching fire as they land.

He paused, stopped, and sat after spinning round three times with its head bowed, and his arms stretched out by his sides. He sat at a distant in front of me, I watched as he unraveled the leaves, held together with ropes and twigs.
I heard screams escape, and watched as living things crawled out of the dead mountain of leaves. He was saying things I could not hear and doing things that I did not understand. I screamed but the breath was lost within me. I tried with all my might to move but my body continued in its ignorance.

'Well, enough of your bizarre description of me', said Safarai with a slightly crooked smile. **'I was trying to save you, trying to see if you were alive,'** he said as his smile quickly turned to a frown and stared motionless at me. He continued:

'Not all that dies are dead and not all that is living is alive. Some use the day for sleeping others for eating; some use the night for resting others for hunting. You

were merely at the boundary of both. You probably had an unfinished calling to do. If not all my screaming and "hopping" as you put it, would have been in vain. I did not save you, I have no power to give or take life only the Creator does.'

'I'm sorry, but I had never seen anything like that before, I mean, you before', I said with a slight hesitation in my voice. Your appearance was quite frightening.'

'So you are Safarai', I said,

'Takunta said I would meet you', I said as a slight joy brewed within me.

'Why do you carry all those things with you, and dressed as you are' I asked. Before he could answer, I said, 'why are you wearing all those clothes, all at once?'

'**Takunta**', he said with a surprising tone in his voice. '**So you have met the wisest wilder-beast that there is, if not the wisest living thing on the grainy sea**', he exclaimed. I have known Takunta for a long while now. "How is he, is he well?" He asked. Before I could reply he answered himself, "Of course he is, he is the great Takunta", any-

way more on him later he said as his attention now fo-
cused on me'

    'Well, these "things" that you see me carrying' he
said, as he shoved the large ruffled leaves in my face is
called the "Ball of Wonder." In it is all that I possess'. He
continued, 'I do not have an abode, not as you would describe it anyway. I live here, and in places that you cannot
see, places you have never been.
I live where I am, and I am where I live. The walls to my
abode stretch beyond the boundary of my eyes. My win-
dow is the high sea, and my doors are forever open. My
roof is the canopy of the great forests and I have water
and food in plenty here in the garden of paradise', he proclaimed, like a proud land owner.'

    I was slightly perplexed because it is either he or I that
was confused because all I could see was the vast wilderness
that surrounded us. He continued:

    'You define your abodes by the small random objects
you place together to create an even smaller space, you have
comfort because your sleeping place nestles in the assembly

of your haphazard materials'. 'I have no need for such clutter', he said as he looked down towards me. Strutting around, he continued, 'for I possess the biggest home, one whose boundary walls I cannot reach with my arms stretched out; one whose walls cannot be breached.'

'Well, I thank you for your help', I replied.

I continued, 'But I have something important to tell you.'

Before I could continue, he turned round in anger and said: **'So how did you get here? Where have you been? You were obviously lost.' 'Tell me your story,'** he demanded.

Chapter Six

TAKUNTA

So I started and said: I spent almost a year traveling before I got to a place that looked like a settlement. I followed the paths of the high light by day, and the night light by night. I watched the migrations of the beasts, and birds, spurred on by an invisible force.

I eat fruits and berries and consumed much leaves. Some were vegetables, others weed; species, and variety untold, and some with lethal after effects. Soon after, I started hunting for meat, rabbits, and the like.

My senses and strength also developed. I was able to form companion with wilder-beasts who guided me to the settlement of the land to the South, and I was able to communicate with all in the animal kingdom, be it those in the blue sea, in the air or those that walk the powder earth. I walked with the kings of the jungle and swam with the creatures of the sea.

Living with the beasts of powder earth, and the mammals of the blue sea, I was told many things, and many secrets were revealed to me. Takunta, the great wilder-beast once asked:

"Why do your people move about on their hind legs and stay so far from the life-source, the grainy sea?"

"Why he asked, do we poke the earth with our branch like hinds, as if we belong not to it and stare at it from aloof as if not related?"

'You forever change your skin like a tree that blossoms and sheds its leaf all in the same day, only to do the same thing the following day.'

"Why is it that we speak to you, yet you respond not?"

"Why is it that we warn you of things, and places yet you pay no heed?"

"Why is it that when we try to communicate with your people, they are forever aggressive?"

"Why is it that you make us work so hard and you begrudgingly give us rest?'

'You entrap the young ones and breed them for food. We forever hear their screams; we hear their cries before the inner lining of their throat are exposed to the air. We stand and witness it as their blood is used to quench the thirsty powder earth. In its greed, it never cries enough, in your want, you never stop feeding it.'

'Our skins you spread for the flies to lay their eggs. Tears fill our eyes as the canker worms burrow the bones of our bones.

'"Why do your people wear our bones, teeth, and skulls around their neck?" 'Oh how often I wished I could breathe life back into them to seize your people by the throat, and watch them drown in air.'

He didn't seem like he wanted me to answer all these questions, even if he did, I wouldn't know where to start. I cannot even remember the first one he asked. Seen that he was content with by silent, I listened on. He continued and said:

'You feed on the young, and enjoy their underdeveloped bones; your teeth shine in the light as you sharpen them on the mature ones. Yet we said nothing, we did nothing. You take from the paradise of plenty as you pleased, to you the unconsumed meat is a waste, but to us, it is a life wasted twice over.

Then, we all decided that this must stop. So every year we all agreed to meet, to gather by the river of Itep, young, and old, large and small, weak and strong. We gathered in our battalions to find a way to fight back. We send messages throughout the land that we needed to raise an army, a strong relentless group whose goal is vengeance on your people.'

'As a group, we considered, like a swarm of bees, we gathered.

'Who will lead the attack?' we asked.

Which ones of us are best to create the most destruction, this became the focus of our contemplation. We measured the night light, and waited on the high light to understand when to attack.'

'The choice was made. We decided to send The Beasts of the Night in your resting period. We scented the air to the far away troupes, birds, and wilder-beasts carried messages far, and wide. The rumbling of our hoofs was not only to get from place to place but was also to carry messages from here to there. Piled up was the anger we felt, none of which you heard, none of which you saw.'

'How can we launch such an attack without letting the people know? We wondered.

This was where Yijugukabu Izaka came in. Although we had the knowledge, we needed the ingenuity of a Dynastic, Izaka, the abandoned-one, was the one to help. After all, we broke the curse that he was under.

'Yes we knew the cure', **he said.**

'Ah,' Safarai interrupted.

'So he told you about Yijugukabu Izaka,' he said with a surprised expression on his face. I paused and looked at him and said:

'Yes'.

Before I could continue, he asked:

'Did he tell you the full story?'

I was puzzled and I asked him, 'Is there more'? He nodded and said: **'Of course there is,'** and continued:

'The spirits he was summoning possessed him
and turned against him. He wanted to be the best hunter
in the Dynasty and was prepared to do anything for it. He
did as instructed, and sacrificed the forbidden beasts of
the wild. Unfortunately, in his desperation, he was not
patient to hear all the instructions properly. Rather than
uttering the good chants, he was doing the opposite.'
'The spirits of the forest were disturbed in their graves
and awoke. All the words he uttered took on a life of their
own, surrounded him, and started attacking him before
he completed his chants. They formed a cloud above
his head, and each word and inscriptions attacked him
in frenzy, cutting, and gauging him. He was chased, and
lifted out of the forest to a place far from the Dynasty's
settlement, and was never seen again.'
'Later, the Dynasties found ground tunnels under
your settlement. It then occurred to them that The Beasts
of the Night tunneled their way from deep in the forest to
your settlement. In their search after Tiron-tamada, they
heard calls for help and sent people to investigate. On

their way, they found a graveyard of bones where the beasts were, and had devoured everything and every-one.'

'Amongst them was a man whose scream they heard, he had been attacked by The Beasts because he had betrayed them. With his last gasps of breath, he explained how The Beasts saved him from his curse as he was chased out of the land of the Dynasty of the North.' 'In return, he had promised to help the beasts overcome their little problem of avoiding the deadly attacks of the guardsmen that had plagued them for generations. He devised the approach by the tunnel and helped plan their attack. His name was Yijugukabu, and it was he that was chanting the forbidden scribes.'

Safarai paused and said in a solemn whisper:

'It was he that planned the attack on the Dynasty of the North.'

After that, he said nothing for a while so I continued where I left the story. 'Takunta continued,' I said:

'You must know that all you do atop the grainy sea, and under the high sea. Each word uttered anywhere, even those on the backs of the smallest flee; we know them all.' 'Did you not know that the branches and the leaves are not deaf, that neither is the rock or the snow blind?'

'We consulted all and found what was used, and what was said. We asked the waterfall of what it saw and listened to the rocks of Sube-mai as to where to go.'

'We found the cure for Izaka but we explained that he must promise to help us in our little issue - the destruction of his own kind. The choice was that either he can stay in his condition where he knew not night or day, friend or foe, the living or the dead; or, if he chooses, he can be cured. Yes, he chose the land of the living, although not for long.'

'You must understand that whatever you do,' Takunta emphasised, 'we know of it, wherever you go, it is not dark to us. We hear all and see all. Your rituals, incantations, and sacrifices that you perform are not new to us. We have seen your wickedness to us and to each other for many generations. Surely, you did not think that only your people can organise, think, and act? You are not the only ones on the three seas you know.'

'The three seas?' I asked.

'Yes,' he replied, with a surprised expression on his face. Then he started to explain:

'You and your people see this place as valleys and mountains, rivers, and hills. You see it as forests and rocks, beasts and mammals, but it does not surprise us. Your kind complicates the simple, yet the simplest things escape them. We have no reason to divide the things that keep us whole. To us, they are all but one thing that is, the sea. The grainy sea, the blue sea, and the high sea, that is all they need to be called.'

'Let me explain,' he continued, sensing that I was confused.

Before, there was only one sea, a young sea. As it grew, it became more powerful as the pressure from its two elder siblings mounted. They were angry that why should the young sea be the heir to all the possessions of the Creator.'

'So night, and day, they waged war against the young sea; terrible vicious war. So much that the high light and the night light could not be seen. Then the Creator sent down the wind to bring peace onto the three siblings, the wind battled but could not resolve them. Then the Creator sent the rain, it came heavily but could not save them. The Creator sent the thunder, and still it could not settle their passionate anger, then the Creator sent the rocks. Rocks of all shape, and sizes but it too battle to no avail. Then the Creator sent the tree, and said, go and hold back the grainy sea from the blue sea with your roots in the earth, separate them above it with your trunk. Hold up the third sea over your head and push the other two apart with your leaves and branches.'

'So the tree sat on the rocks and held back the grainy sea and the blue sea from each other. It kept the rain on one side, and the wind, and the air on the other. But thunder it could not control, its fury was too much. So until this day although the three siblings are separated, thunder still rages on. That is why its arrival is always that of anger, preceded by dark clouds as it makes its entry; stinging the grainy sea, the blue sea, and the high sea as a sign of retribution.'

'So Takunta,' I said, 'these rocks have ears and these leafs are befitted with eyes?'

The very thought stilled with me shudder. Surely rocks cannot converse neither can a branch talk.'

'Takunta is lying', I murmured to myself so that he did not hear me, 'he must be,' I declared to myself.

'Imagine, a talking tree . . .?' Well there is only one thing to do that is to go, and speak to a tree, and question the pebbles. I will ask the sheaves of grass what they have seen, and consult with the lakes all they have heard.

'Surely it cannot be', I said to myself again.

'But why not', said a quite, clear voice in my head.

Come to think about it, I have been conversing with Takunta, the great wilder-beast, and have befriended the great whales of the deep, and rode on the back of eagles.

'But it cannot be', I said, trying not to convince myself of the impossible. Rocks are not alive, and the trees are gifted not with voices.'

'They have no life . . . yet they are alive,'

'They have no eyes, yet they . . . No. No. They cannot see.'

'Let me think about this I said to myself. If I stand still for 50 years does that mean that I cannot move because I have not moved or if I utter not a voice in a lifespan does that mean that I cannot speak because I have not spoken?'

'If I have eyes to see and other cannot see my eyes does that mean I cannot see or is it they that cannot see that I see them, and do not know the gift I possess?'

'What if my eyes were different to those they are accustomed to, do I still have eyes?'
'Can I see, even though they know not that I can? . . .'

'What I'm I talking about, trees do not have eyes. If this was so, they will see like my people, if they had feet, they will match like the wilder-beasts.'

Takunta looked at me and said:

'Well, that is interesting. But surely the voice is not only used for speaking but for communicating.'

I replied him and said:

'But surely, every word spoken is communication, if not then what is its purpose? Takunta did not answer me. Whether he thought all this was too much for me to understand, or

that I was correct, he did not comment, he just continued as if
I never spoke.'

'So you have never seen a tree dance or see its leaves
shimmer to the rhythms of nature?'

'But a tree waving in the wind is not dancing. Trees just
grow, they do not know what they do, they just grow, upwards,
taller, and bigger . . .'

'So you are saying that they move yet they know not
where they go; that they talk but know not what they say?'

'Trees and rocks stay put. They do not move, neither do
they talk, stop trying to confuse me' I screamed.

'Confusion' he replied, 'is only a temporary, uncomfortable state of mind where we chose to refuse others ideas
because it contradicts ours...'

'So Takunta, how do you know that they talk?' I asked
in my dismay.

'Uhm, so you are asking a wilder-beast? You are conversing with one that utters no knowledge, but surely beasts do not talk. They only grunt, surely they lack that power of the intellect, remember. Do you know that Safarai has five wives?'

Like he knew I was struggling to grasp the idea, and therefore changed it to one I could understand. To hide my ignorance, I quickly shouted:

'We are discussing how rocks talk, and you change the subject?' Unfortunately for me, the latter idea was even more complicated. I tried to hold on but I just kept slipping down the slope of knowledge. However, what he was going to explain confirmed my place at the foot of the hill of wisdom; I had never heard such things before. So I said:

'What or who is Safarai, and why tell me about how many wives he has? I do not even know him.'

'You will soon meet him', he said calmly. 'Yes, he is married to five wives, six to be precise. The memory of the sixth fails me; insignificant she is not, reasons of which I will explain, but he is married to five wives.'

'Not that one is not enough, not that the love each has for him is inadequate, but that each offer different love; for he craves different needs. He craves different desires of love; different attention, different understanding, patience, beauty, passion - indeed they all possess it, it is their seasonal waves which he could not content. Whilst one in her season bathes in understanding and passion, her beauty and attention wane towards him.'

'Why I asked myself, does his attention slip by like the passage of time, why did he muddy his delicate jewels? I know not. But that which I know is that which he trusts, that which he trusts is that which he does, that which he does is indeed that which he acts.'

'Without a doubt, he holds all of them precious. Closer to him they all are than the hairs on his body. Each has indeed etched their tracks of affection in his heart, with their eloquent meandering routes. They delight in the joy that they confuse those looking in, those they call the "Outsiders" that do not understand them. Some of his wives he married by tradition, others through choice. He married late, he married young, he married many so he can feel the depth of love many times over.'

'He married the hot tempered; he married cold mannered, he married the slow, and married the fast. He married once, he married twice, and more so that he can have more joy.'

'He is married to the high light, and to the night light.'

'He is married to the tree and the hill.'

'He is married to the fire and to the rain.'

This is the reason why he wonders. As he spends time with one the others call out to him, their beauty, he yearns, their cries he cannot deny; their jealousy he cannot see.'

'Safarai, a person, is married to the night light. Did I hear you correctly, and the rain? I said in a tone of disgust and curiosity. Unphased by my reaction, Takunta continued:

'He is the only person that can harness all the strength from all these elements. The Creator gave him the gift but at a cost - that he will not have a fixed abode. He will roam the land been neither man nor beast, not only that, because of his great gifts, he is plagued with the battle of doubt and confusion which only he can resolve. We all have these in us, but the greater we become, the greater things we look to achieve, the greater, and louder the voices of doubt becomes.'

'You see,' Takunta said as he pointed to his head,

'The greatest battle we all face is not what is out there, rather what is in here.'

I stood up quickly, roused by my astonishment. However, Takunta continued as if what he had just said was a fleeting comment.

'I tell you,' he continued, 'I have seen trees move, and living things stand still like the tree of Sube. Surely you know about Zumete, where your people become tree-like in order to trap preys.'

'Yes, the Zumete, but that was just a story', I said, as I tried to come to grips with all that I have been hearing. My head began to spin again, convinced that all this was a dream. As if he knew what I was thinking, Takunta looked at me and said:

'No, this is not a dream.'

I looked at him, my eye wide open, still I saw nothing; I opened my mind, but still I could not understand. As if in denial, like he had not said anything to me, he continued:

'Uhm, that is correct,' replied Takunta. 'What you do not know knows you, and those that you think you know, you know them not,' he acclaimed.

'Many millennia's ago,' he continued, 'your people made an agreement with the trees. That if the trees gave them the protection they need, they will honour them by giving them part of their senses every time they perform the Zumete. So, the great trees of the past got together, and decided on what it is from humankind they wanted.'

'They chose two things: seeing and walking. For they have roots that can be like feet, branches, and leaves that can be like eyes. Your people agreed and said that only particular types of a tree will be able to use these talents, a smaller selection still will be able to use both abilities. It got to a stage where people and trees got so close that they started intermarrying. I guess Safarai is one of the last of that generation', he said with a slight sadness of expression on his face.'

With a renewed enthusiasm he continued:

'There was a great drought on the grainy sea, and no trees could bear leaves or fruits; many died. However, a young girl pleaded with a tree. She promised to find it water and prune it, keep its surroundings tidy, and keep the stinging hornets off its trunks, and branches.

Everyday she did as she promised to the extent that the tree was the only one left, and it eventually bore fruits for the girl everyday. As a result, they both survived so she stayed. In the evening, she would lay by its roots, and the tree protected her and covered her with its leaves. This went on for several years until one day, she disappeared.'

'Some believed that she became part of the tree, others say that she lives in the tree, some said she died. Sometimes when the night light is high, our ancestors believe that she comes out at night in her full green splendour as her eyes shine like rare clear stones. We believe that she protects the forests, and trees from harm.'

'Some elder wilder-beasts and birds said they have seen her go to the high sea to plead with the Creator when the high light is too hot or the rain is too strong. She is the Goddess of the Trees. She granted your people a place of safety, and rest during the season of the first high waters. This is why the Dynasty of the South have made their abode there. They said they love living in the bosoms of the Goddess.'

Chapter Seven

REMEMBER

Remember the strong couple off the land,
The King with fire in his breath,
And Ice on his eyes.

His voice has power,
It shakes and trembles all,
His words are hot and harsh,
But forgiving.

The King's words bring life,
They bring new life,
They never fail.

Remember his Queen,

Her heart is calm with peace,
She flows gently,
Like a river.

They all gather in her bosom for knowledge,
For her mind is beautiful,
She is forever thinking of paradise.

Remember the King and the Queen,
They both breathe and speak life
But hurry,
For they may change their words.

Remember, remember. . .

Mother, 'Is that you?'

Mother, what does this mean? I do not understand.

'Which King, what Queen?' Mother, mother. . .

Chapter Eight

CHAMBERS OF DREAMS

Safarai seemed to be patient and encouraged me to talk. Whether he was amused or interested, I could not work out the expression on his face. Then he started to unwrap his Ball of Wonder. I paused as if to say 'What is that?' I looked on as he started bringing out several objects of varying sizes; some looked like bones of varying texture and lengths. Some look as if they were rotten, whilst others looked like he had tied random, discarded objects together in a hurry. Noticing that it had gone quite, and I was no longer talking, he said:

'Continue, continue . . .'

With his head bowed to the ground. Now, and then,

his face will look serious, as if concentrating on something. At
other times he would break out into a dramatic choking laugh
interrupted with sharp silence. Confused as to what to do, I
stared with curiosity. Without even looking at me, he shouted
again:

'Continue I say, continue. . .'

So I decided to tell him the two dreams I had. I said:

'Through my journey, a number of secrets were revealed to me, and I was shown many visions. I learned the
great sounds of the whale, and they revealed the mighty power of sound to me. In my wondering, visions became dreams,
dreams became nightmares, nightmares became reality; some
days were just an extension of my slumbering stupor.

I saw images and heard sounds, and many voices filled my
head. Some of the dreams I had forgotten by the time I awoke,
some I wish I could forget, some can never escape me, whilst
others I knew not their meaning.'

'In one of them,' I continued, 'I was in a valley, and its
mountains on both sides were far away . . .'

But as I tried to continue, he started arranging the objects that were in his Ball of Wonder onto the ground. Using them to make patterns, some of them looked like images of birds or mountains, others I could not make out, maybe because they were upside down. This time he stopped. Raised his head slowly, and looked up at me angrily. Before he said anything else, I knew what he was going to say, so I continued again.

'At a distance' I said, 'I saw what I thought was the second high-light, as it glimmered, and shinned like a large precious stone object. I moved closer to it, and its shape revealed itself to me, it was a large, gold decorated drinking vessel. Its rim almost touched the high sea, and the large circular base it stood on was almost my height. Its surface was covered with inscriptions, symbols, and signs all of which I could not understand. At random intervals, studs of what looked like precious beautiful stones interrupted each set of images, they were like large shinning pebble stones.'

It was at this point that Safarai stopped what he was doing, and repeated some of the things I just said with some other random words slowly:

'The gold goblet of the Gira . . . The sacred inscriptions . . . Ancestral names of the Walalas . . .'

This time I paused and asked him:

'What is the Gira' and

'What or who is the Walalas?'

He looked up and said:

'I will tell you later my son,' 'Continue', he shouted.
So I did and said:

'As I walked around the goblet, my gold reflection followed me slowly. I looked up the stem of it, yet more inscriptions, but these once I could not see properly for they were too far towards the high sea. As I walked around its splendour, for no apparent reason it started to tilt and fall.

So I ran as to brace its fall, even though I could not even budge the plinth it stood on. I was startled when I realised that the faster I ran the faster the goblet fell, when I slowed it slowed, but was still falling.

'What is this' I said to myself. Then, from above, I saw that something was spilling from it, it looked like molten the hot flowing river as the liquid reflected the high light and the vessel it spilled from.

Then in a moment, it started to pour uncontrollable, and the cup shifted and tilted even more. It soon became apparent that this was indeed the juice of the pressed grapes, sweet red water. So I ran as fast as I could but the sweet liquid poured even more.

'Aah, the red river of the Murulis, nobody can stop it . . . nobody,'

He whispered again before a small smile crawled sluggishly across his tired face. Then I continued. 'The red torrent swept me off my feet and brought me to the ground. In the panic, I tried to stay afloat, and swim to safety but I was covered, drowning in the warm juice.'

'Ha ha, hee heee', he laughed for no reason, then whispered again 'NOBODY . . .'

I was now getting used to his interruptions, and the weird world he seemed to be living in. So I decided to just keep talking without having to wait for him to shout: 'continue'.

I looked on as he spat on branches, and scattered a handful of bones, pushing, and moving each in turn. Confused as to what he was doing, I continued and said:

'Soon the valley was filled to the rim. I looked from a distance and the cup continued to fall, and spill even more. Suddenly, all around me, I saw bodies of people and animals floating. Numerous dead bodies and limbs flowed past me like been washed downstream in a river. Some were floating face up, some face down. Some had eyes missing, whilst others had their mouths open with no teeth. A floating, de-fleshed head came crashing towards me, I panicked and woke up.

'You seem to have quite a gift', he said, 'quite special gifts . . .'

I was going to stop there, and ask him what he was doing, and why he acting so awkward, but as if he knew there was more; he paused and kept quiet, his eye fixed to the abstract diagram he had just created in front of him, and then waited for me to continue, so I preceded and said:

'Covered in sweat, I vomited the settled waters in my bowels, with my back ached over, coughing, spitting, and crying.

    'What have I just witnessed,' I asked myself, 'what a strange, disturbing dream, I said.'

    'I sat upright disturbed by what I had seen only to hear the knock on the door.

    'Ahh, pain, it is you again', I said to myself.
'Why torture me in bits you beast? I asked as if it had a life of its own. Even when I try to escape your reach of sting with a little daydream, you bring me back again in the blink of an eye.' 'I am torn' I said in anguish. 'Half of me is in this body, the other is in your grasp, you jealous, angry monster.' Why can you not just leave me be?' I asked as if it had ears.

    'Oh, how much I wish that I were like the Dynasty of the East in real life like the story of my father. I will pull you out of me, and stomp on you until you were buried deeper than the deepest tree roots. If you appear again, I will chase you until you fall tired, and let you experience the anguish of being hounded.' My face frowned, teeth gritted, and saliva sprayed and drooled from my lips and said, 'then I will grip you by the throat with my hands, and squeeze the very life from you and see how you like it.'

'Oh, if only the Choord bird too was here. I will say with a beaming smile, "take me on your wings, and fly me to paradise; let us go to the banquet of the Dynasty of the East and feast like Kings"'. 'We will fly over the hills, and mountains, and be glad that I am leaving you behind.'

'Oh it is no use,' I said, as my grin turned sour again. I admitted to myself that 'fake foods only feed fake hunger, and dreaming that one has eaten never fills the belly in real life.'

'I fell, face first to the ground and my charred lips gathered up the grainy sea again. To my surprise, as quickly as the hunger came, it disappeared again, and deep slumber came over me. I tried to stay awake but the warm embrace of sleep held me gently again, as I curled like a new-born in its caring, soft oversized arms.'

'In another dream,' I said, 'I listened but heard no sounds, no faint familiar voice, not even a noise that could move the heart to sing'. 'My senses were now open to the surroundings. I felt the smallest mammal of the sea and saw the first places of settlement in the waters.

'Aah, the Abyss of Alvi . . .'

'I snapped out of my slumber, woke, and realised that I was now like them - a mammal with fins, and tails. Breathing underwater with ease, plunging to depths of darkness I never before witnessed. I heard a voice that said he will "continue to call me until I returned to their midst", that I was, "destined to carry my father's voice". It was then that I realised what I had become.'

'Aah, the seven changes of Walalas . . .'

'I shook my flattened, joined fingers for them to regain their form. I coughed to remove the waters from my lungs but they were all foolish acts. I longed to quench my lungs with air again. I crave to feel the sweat run down my face and to stomp on the grainy sea, and for it to push me back again. I wanted to feel the rising of the low high light, and watch, and hear the birds dance and sing.

I wanted to pick the sweet berries in the thick violent bush and sit by the rocks of Uzeleto. I looked up to the high sea and long to be closer to the Creator. Amidst my thoughts came a strong current sweeping all that was in its path. On land, I traveled for a purpose and I go to random places because I chose to. Now, all I see is the deep dark blue sea with no ground, no landmarks, or trees. All I did was to drift in the reef.'

Then I stopped, but this time Safarai did not seem concerned about my silence anymore, he was more interested in the fire he was making. As the wind blew, the fire grew. I sat and watched it engulf. Its flames changed colours like the setting of the high light. Its heat radiated as I watched it burn in stages, I was almost enchanted by it.

For the first time in a while, Safarai started to talk and continued in his slow, whispery voice, he said:

'The way a fire behaves must be one of the most beautiful, fragile, yet frightening thing there is. Fire, that enigmatic, and at the same time known element, still manages to pervade, and outwit us. Heat is possibly more uncomfortable than the cold, whilst one can brush fallen snow off the shoulder or ignore it and watch it melt. The same playfulness does not mingle with its relative; fire offers no luxury of random activity. Even the slow caress

of its heat is one that is to be watched closely.'

He continued, 'similar to how the blue sea beck-
ons one to come in. Its soft form, and the deep blues and
shimmering greys; the continual blinking of its surface,
the caress of its gentle sway as the ripples draws one-
in. Gradually it feels like the ground is too cruel on the
foot, and joints. The body and mind imagine trading it
for something softer; the water. Its continual rhythmic
sounds, and shifting patterns block everything out. The
eyes and mind are now on nothing else but just diving-in.
The head full of romantic memories of bathing, and swimming. On a cold day, it is tempting, on a hot day, resist-
ance does not register in the psyche.'

'Similar to the feeling of walking along a cliff edge
- one eye on the path, the other down at the bottom of the
cliff, the mind already traveled the journey backward and
forwards numerous times. The body left suspended at
the edge, the mind already fallen as the stomach churns,
imagining the force that would be experienced, wondering whether the head or the feet will lead the fall first. The
wind in the face, and imagining how long it would take to
reach the bottom.'

'Then at an instance, the mind wonders back to the edge of the cliff, grip tightened, taking small steps as if learning to walk again. The body's weight deliberately overloaded to one side, favouring the solid ground to the attempt to take off and fly. The sudden jerks of the waist are an unwanted complication. The mind in a battle between been free and holding on to reality but soon concludes, preferring to stay on the higher ground.'

Before he began speaking, the fire was burning slowly, and calmly. Then everything began heating up and caught fire at random, all of a sudden, the fire reached its peak; it seemed invigorated and alive as if it was hearing the voice of Safarai. I watched as the little flame had dramatically turned to an island of fire. On the other side of the flames, I saw Safarai, throwing things into it, and blowing the smoke into my face as the noise of the fire masked his voice. With my eyes stinging with the smoke, I thought that I saw him in the fire itself, standing, looking at me with another figure as they both danced with the flames.

My eyes watered again, I wiped them, and they watered again, this time as I cleared the tears the second time, I knew not what came over me as I started talking uncontrollably. Words it seemed were running out of my mouth by themselves, it became difficult putting a few coherent words together as I said to him, 'I have a confession to make.'

'What is this you are saying, I understand not. Why are you polluting our ancestor's tongue with gibberish? Safarai responded.'

'Gibberish, what do you mean?' I replied.

'You are doing it again' he said, 'what has happened to your tongue, you were not talking like this a little while ago? he said.

'Yes, but I do not understand. I am speaking perfectly well, 'am I not,' I asked but no response came. I had been on grainy sea for seven years when Tiron-tamada happened, and all I knew and loved shattered. I am sorry that I do not speak as well as you but I am only eight years old, what do you expect? I asked in an angry voice.'

'Eight years old!' Safarai repeated with great astonish-ment and then said nothing after that.

So I replied, 'yes,' and continued:

'The event happened last year, and I have been try-ing to find my way around to see or speak to someone with no success.'

He continued to look at me with amazement. Then it dawned on me that maybe my speech is not as good as it should be. In the past year or so, I have not seen or spoken to any of our people. All I have had for a company are the wilder-beasts, the birds of the high sea, the mam-mal of the blue sea. But then, why is it now that suddenly he cannot understand me, we have been talking all this while and he had said nothing until now.

I paused as I thought that maybe I am not sound-ing as I think I am . . . Or maybe, maybe it is the smoke in my lungs . . .

'Has he transported me back to when I was in my youth? . . .'

'Is he making me say things I did not want to say? . . .'

'What has he done to me? . . .'

'What was he putting in the fire? . . .'

'What are you doing to me?' I must have mumbled.

All these questions I could not answer, but something was certain, I could not stop talking. The more I tried to stop, the harder it became not to speak.

'Wait, wait, wait, you speak no sense, and your wind blow with no direction' Safarai said.

'Well, you have done it now or should I say, you have done it, a-g-a-i-n . . .'

'Failure you are back. . .' said Safarai.

'Yes Condemned, it is wise for you to notice the obvious. You take a perfectly formed person, and turn him into this scattering, chattering, and confused buffoon.

No wonder you were so eager to help. I can see the resemblance; you both utter the divine breath but your battering of the wind offers no breeze of intelligence. Though you displace the invisible powers, your colouring still goes unnoticed, you speak yet no one understands.'

'Greetings to you,' I said to the visitor that just joined us. 'Are you Safarai's friend or relative,' I asked. He did not answer me, instead, he said:

'Ha ha ha, I have no business with you, it is this waste of life that I seek to converse. Curse be to all the seeds from his loin from this life to the afterlife. He shall not prosper, he will not prosper, he must not prosper, him, and his children will not prosper. Curse be to the day that he was born, cursed also to the day he shall be no more.'

'I hope that the high light does not shine on him, and the waters reject his body. I hope the night light becomes his enemy, and the rain to be like fire upon his skin; oh air, come, and be his greatest adversary.'

'I hope the ground that he walks on traps him, and the cool breeze never find him. Open, ground I command, and swallow him. I hope the food he eats chokes him, and his meals never finds him on time. I command that when it is hot, that it is cold to him, and all things that are cold to scold him.'

'What is this?' I asked, with what they would have considered a naïve voice. I was surprised and said:
'How could you be saying all these things to him, you have only just arrived and you a wishing for the ground to swallow him.' Well, I knew not their past relations and their discussion was of no interest to me. More importantly, the words of the dream in me seemed to be burning my lips so I turned to Safarai and said to him again:

'I have something to tell you'.

'I still understand not fully a word that you utter, but we will come back to that. But I think you asked who Failure was . . .'

'I have a name and it is not Failure, you know that - The Mad One. You never cease to amaze me. You deny those that you know and those that know you want nothing to do with you when you call them . . .'

'As I was saying, Failure is like a bad spirit that forever follows . . .'

'*How dare you interrupt me? From today, all favours will be an interruption in your life. The very life will interrupt you and your soul; interruption will be at your rising, interruption at your resting place, nothing good will intersect you . . .*'

'I called it so to remind myself that no matter what he utters, however logical its speech may seem, his intents are always malice. Therefore, I pay no attention to anything he says, however, condescending his tongue.'

'*It is you whose tongue should be cut off, need I say more. Cut off I say, as the life of day when the night comes; cut off as the blue sea is from the high sea; cut off you shall be, all cut, and cut off.*'
'*Look at your polluted work, your new apprentice, singing beautiful songs to your ears, I saw you nodding rhythmically to his confusing gibberish.*'

'Like I said, ignore him at all times, at all costs, all will be explained later. Now you, why do you utter your voice the way you do. Although you utter your words, I still hear not what you say.'

I nodded my head as if I knew what they were both arguing about. Nevertheless, the longer I waited the hotter the words seem to get in my mouth. 'Please,' I shouted, 'you have to listen, and understand me.' Before I could continue Safarai interrupted me and said:

'Each word you utter afflicts my very soul and burns my very being. When you talk, it is like fastening my lips to the volcano and its hot river filling the empty chambers of my mouth. I see that you are desperate to tell me something; eager to inform me. The breath you utter I see; the words you impart I hear not.

'What could be so urgent to tell when all that was alive have perished? What is it I wonder will you say that will let me experience the beautiful land in its fullest again. What is it I wonder that will let me experience the beautiful Paradise that is now lost. Now that the high light refuses to make a stand, and has become a recluse, and the night light has lost its incentive to shine with the stars.'

'What is it I ask, now that the Dynasties and the animal kingdom have disappeared? The beast's nightly hymns are replaced with harrowing echoes; the fluttering in the high sea of the birds is now replaced by the hissing of the Lava as it battles the blue sea. What can you utter that will bring back the Sube tree and the calming words of the streams? What can you say that will bring back the strength of the people from the East, the beauty of the Dynasties of the West or revive the indigenous people of the South?'

'Oh Valley of Isalamata, where are you gone? The place of oasis by the river Rutenoi-pyepe, marking the point of the South and the North of the land. The Valley where the peaceful serene land lies, with its back, turned to the High Mountain and lava encrusted landscape of the West. The grainy sea of the East to its front; to the right, the expanse of the Great Plains of the South; and to the left, the Paradise of the North. Oh, Valley of knowledge, where all gather for educating, for debate, for discussion. You brought light to the minds of the young Dynasties and was proud of your amphitheatres and great edifices.

You gave shelter from the environment, and quietness unfounded anywhere else in the land resided in your heart. Your banks and ridges lined with diverse fruits and vegetation, as river Rutenoi-pyepe slowly drifts by.

'Oh Mouth of Incabih, who quieted your voice? You, the place of the shortest crossing distance between the land of the South and the East; and separate the warm South and the cold North. You that held great turbulent between your cheeks and only allow crossings when your anger has passed.
The great, Danda Incabih made your lips his home and the Sustegaro fishes hide in you for protection from them. The Dynasties, the beasts and the Sustegaro all play the game of death on your tongue; one wrong move and the hunter becomes the hunted. Oh, Danda Incabih for such a large mammal why dance in shallow waters with one of the smallest fishes in the river.'

Hills of Sandosa, we miss watching water dance up, onto and over your face; the only place where water travels up the mountain face. The algae on your face lure them, only to release them atop, as they go crashing down as the mighty waterfall.

You hold the great powerful waters at your feet and channel them slowly at your toes. You erupt and flood the land to the South and force the Dynasties to live on the necks of the Sube-mai tree for a quarter of the year. They concede as land become sea; the young ones love you best. They revel and say; they love your work, it is the dramatic change you bring; that made them stay first.

'Sube-mai trees never thought you could ever hide. As the tallest tree, that is why the South loves you best. Tall large and strong, as you smile at the top. You tower your surroundings and roots fastened to the foundation of the land. Only you can be seen at the flooding of the Dynasties, your head in the clouds, whispering to the Creator. You witnessed the birth of all this; before their King and Queen. It is no surprise; you are the Creators best-loved.'

'Where are you Mount Sumbiti, the place of fire and heat and hot flowing river? When you visit, no one can refuse you passage. You are a force that cannot be tamed; a beast that does not listen. The Dynasty of the South are settled out of reach; those of the East are glad when your fury is over; those of the North are happy that they do not have to contend with you.

You indeed were a fearful and dreadful place. To your right, the hot pouring river; to your left, Mount Bila-guro, the coldest place on the land. But still, you are forgiving. To the far West of the land, the Dynasty found a way to form settle and inhabit your hills. They found ways of living with your moods.'

'The mystical Choord is nowhere to be found. The beautiful Great Plains and the consuming waters of the South, to the intricate carvings of stone, ice, and wood are now but a memory. The rocky ravines, and the most beautiful people in the land vanished. We may never meet the great philosophers again.'

'The darkness has replaced the power of the high light; beasts and plants alike are all gone; the great places of the land are lost. Oh come back, the Valley of Isalamata; make an appearance, the grainy sea to the East.

Oh Mouth of Incabih, why keep silent . . .'

'Please Safarai, you need to listen,' I said, as I interrupted him. 'I wanted to teach them a lesson' I screamed. I
seemed to have got his attention as he replied:

'Teach who, and why? He replied.

Burdened with my pregnant tongue I said, 'I was in the
wilderness for a long time, and no one cared for me, all in their
weak, half hearted search for me. I sat on the backs of birds
and clung to the under belly of wilder-beasts, as we galloped
through the forest. I saw those they sent to look for me. I saw
them getting bored and going for a swim in the Iskoyi Lake.
I watched as they lay fast asleep under the tree of Febo, only
to be awakened from their slumber with a tickle on the nose
by the leaf I was holding, but by the time they woke, I could
not be seen. I wanted them to feel the loss I had felt when the
sight of my love, Jelë, was taken from her.'

'Aah, the blind girl Jelë, so you knew her',

Safarai replied as he looked down, and away from me pondering on what I just said. Now that I had his attention I quickly spoke:

'She was my love, and we lived in the same settlement. She lived a short walk from our abode. We had promised to be man, and wife, even though we knew not what it meant. None of that matters anymore anyway since I lost her in the event of Tiron-tamada.'

'It was impossible to escape even if you were a man, but for a young girl with no sight, only the Creator knows the ordeal she must have gone through. I remembered how she cared for her younger brothers, I found her endearing, and so beautiful, so caring.'

'For it to have ended like it did for her was most unjustified' I said as I clenched my fist tighter. Anyway, the confession, I am sorry, so sorry, if only I knew. 'If only. . .'

'Speak your mind, repressed expression only burdens the heart, and poisons the belly, which it seems to be doing to you.'

'It is the event of Shunku-shunku, it is all my fault . . .'

'It could not be. It was the result of fighting between the Dynasties that caused it . . .'

'That maybe so, but I may have had a part to play in orchestrating it . . .'

'Orchestrating the Shunku-shunku, you are but confused, surely . . .'

'Yes indeed, just like you, his master. You are not to blame; it is this Thing that is to be accountable. Did I not say that nothing well ever comes out of your hands? You tainted the just, and confused the upright, you . . .'

'No, he actually helped me.'

'You are indeed as confused as he is . . .'

'I had a dream, I had many dreams, and it is only now that it is starting to make sense. The dream was... I paused as

I realised what just became clear to me. I continued, it was about the Single rule, and it was going to anger the Creator. I saw how he was to vent his anger, and divide the settlements, and their land. In the dream, there were four groups, I mean settlement . . .'

'Settlements, do you not mean Dynasties...'

'Dynasties?'

'Yes, settlements refer to where a group of people live; the people themselves are called Dynasties.'

'Dynasties . . .'

'Do you want to repeat it again because I did not hear you say 'Dynasties' at the other two occasions?'

'Dynasties . . . It was then that I remembered the story my father told before the Tiron-tamada . . . It is only now that I am realising that it may not be a mere story at all. That he was teaching us the history of our people, our ancestors, our

Dynasties.' So I turned to Safarai quickly and asked,

'Is there such a thing as a Choord bird like you said?'

'Did our people live to the North, the East, the West, and the South? And do you know about the Seven Pillars of Strength?'

'Yes of course' he answered, **'why do you ask?'** he replied.

I heard his question but I could not answer him. Then I asked him another question: 'Were our people the great philosophers you mentioned earlier, and were the Dynasties of the South singers, dancers, and story tellers?'

'Yes of course,' he answered again and continued. **'They danced and sang all the time, regardless if they were happy or sad.'** He added, **'even when they spoke'** . . . I completed his sentence for him and said '. . . it is as if they are singing'.

Safarai laughed for the first time. His teeth were all scattered, crusty and burnt. Whether he had been eating rocks or rocks had eaten his teeth I do not know. The ones that escaped that abuse were the lucky ones - they were missing. He asked me how I knew what he was going to say. He looked at me and asked if I was feeling all right. I think he must have realised that something had just come over me.

I must have stumbled even more in my speech as I tried to continue. The smoke still burned within me as I said in a panic 'the Single rule,' 'the Single rule,' I repeated and then continued:

'I saw that for the very first time the Dynasties will see each other as inferior to the point that even elder men and women will deny that they had any connection with other Dynasties. As I said the word "Dynasties", the smoke seemed to clear from my head and I said:

'. . . The second high light, the great cup . . .'

'. . . That is it. I have just realised; the cup represented the people . . .'

'. . . Inscriptions . . .'

'. . . The inscriptions are all the names our Dynasties . . .'

'. . . The water of the pressed grapes, the red water is not water at all but blood . . .'

'. . . The blood of our people, of the wilder-beasts, and the animal kingdom . . .'

'. . . It was not juice at all . . .'

'. . . There was going to be large amounts of . . .'

'. . . Blood spilled in the valley . . .'

'. . . That is, the grainy sea . . .'

'. . . The golden goblet . . .'

'. . . The goblet is what holds all living things together . . .'

'. . . That is, life itself . . .,'

The last few words faded on my tongue as I felt a great hollow within me.

Safarai looked. Rather than being annoyed by my rambling speech, he smiled. He said:

'That was what I was saying to you earlier when I said: "the gold goblet of the Gira"; that meant the life form made by the Creator; "the sacred inscriptions", that is, the list of all living things; and "the ancestral names of the Walalas", "Walalas" means people, our people.'

With a tone of concern in his voice, he asked me again:

'Is everything all right with you?'

This time, it was my turn to be silent. I stared at him, and my mind went blank. Then I remembered the dream that I had when I was like a fish, and shaking my fins so that they become fingers again. Then the words came back to me again:

'I heard a voice that said they will continue to call me until I returned to their midst,' that I was 'destined to carry my father's voice'.

'Was it you that said that Safarai?' I asked. He grinned again, surprised with my recollection.

'All these flash backs you are having kid,' he said, **'hope you did not see me shaking and crying,'** he laughed aloud.

'That is it' I said, as I tried to stop the tears blurring my vision. I wiped it with my left hand then my right but neither seemed to help.

'You were trying to save me,' I said. The first time I saw you, 'you were trying to save my life. I remembered it been noisy, and I felt dizzy. Everything was just going round, and round. I could not understand what was happening, it was not until when the noise stopped that I started feeling the pain.' Then I continued to tell him the dream and said:

'In the dream I saw that there was an event to anger the Creator and bring to question all of which was created. The Maker was to show his wrath; divide the Dynasty and their land. For the first time they would perceive others as inferior And become weary of each other to the point that they will almost deny ties with other Dynasties.

They became insular, and gradually perished. They became divided and as a result, they started emulating, and creating for themselves the talents, and gifts other Dynasties once possessed, whilst never fully succeeding. Not only were they not able to attain this, they also lost their own natural abilities. Disarray poisoned them, and they never regained their original ancestral blessings. Even as adaptive as they were, their powers faded; knowledge eroded.'

'Although they had the skills to predict the weather, they were never accurate. When they launched their spears, and arrows, they now regularly miss the target. Before, they summoned the rain in dry season, the cool wind in the heat of the day, and extended the duration of the high light, and the night light - all this was lost.'

'The Dynasty of the East that are usually in hibernation for a quarter of a year had to change their living patterns. They were unable to get the rest they needed to re-invigorate themselves. The beasts that were once helpful to the Dynasties no longer did so; they were now forced to help them.

The relationship between them changed as a result, tools, and techniques were developed to make the wilderbeasts obey them. The knowledge of what was good for the species of the land; the high sea and the blue sea were now turned and used to the advantage of each Dynasty.

In the past, Kings and leaders of each Dynasty requested for help and assistance from other Dynasties, now other ways of acquiring these services were sought. Rules were devised and other Dynasties both young and old were fraudulently taken and punished. Soon other Dynasties followed their pattern of behaviour, for fear of not wanting to be the victim of others. Now, blinded in hearts and mind, each was as guilty as the other. Individual achievements were put before the collective. For the first time, one Dynasty wanted to rule all. The realization that they were all from the same Dynasty pervaded them. Consequently, any facial, and body feature that were different from other Dynasties became a cause for mockery and reason for execution.'

'The Creator was angry about the way the Dynasties had turned to malice. The answer was simple: greed, power; jealousy and hatred. It became a disease that could not be cured; an ailment seemingly with no remedy. The Creator allowed the Dynasties to wallow in their misfortunes, and ill judgements. Saddened by what has happened, he was not going to let this generation go unpunished. They were to realise that there is power beyond power, knowledge beyond the wise and understanding and visions that span beyond eternity'

'In the process, the Dynasty of the West that were the most beautiful changed for the worse, and could no longer bear to look at their own reflections. The Queen of the Dynasty of the West was unable to confront her own image in her mirror. On one occasion, she went to the blue sea, when the wondering stars lit the night and the night light coloured all. She peered into the blue sea at the edge of the rock, and the blue sea revolted.

It lashed at the cliffs, and from then on, it was unsettled forever more. It turned into a thick state, like the fats of a lamb, and suffocated all living things that dwelt in it. It swallowed all living creatures in it and those that came to quench their thirst, and later spat out their carcasses in disgust. The blue sea became a living monster. Its breath once fresh reeked, and its shoreline full of rotten carcasses.

'The land suffered draught, and also slowly perished. They traded their most valued possessions until they had no more. All their precious stones, fine clothing, gleaming abodes were all but gone. The Dynasty's fine and fair features all perished. Now, scabs, boils, and warts invaded, and disfigured their faces. The disease attacked every surface of their body that light shone on. Resting became painful, and sleeping, impossible.

All things that reflected their image in their homes were either destroyed or traded. The people that were once approachable and full of confidence became recluses. At times no one could be seen outside as people walked through their land by day. The affliction made them beings of the night. Even when the night light was not shinning, it was still unbearable for them. They traded at night to avoid the preying eyes of others, and wrapped up their bodies and faces as if in

Jelë

disguise. For them, night became day and day like night.'

'They paid higher prices for their goods and supplies because other Dynasties were not willing to trade with them. For the night belonged to beasts of all kinds; daytime was for the people. It is a rule that all are aware of, and one that had been adhered to by all. Attacks ran rife on the people by wilder-beasts whom became aware of the recent movements of the Dynasties, particularly paths leading to the West of the land.'

'Since the trading activities of the Dynasties of the North came to a halt. Those that were affected the most were the Dynasty of the West and those of the East for the previous year's fewer beasts were taken for meat. Season after season all dwindled and therefore sought alternative means.'

'The Rutenoi-pyepe river, a life source and trading channel between the East and the West dried-up. As a result, they decided to come together and form a solution. Both Dynasties knew that the Dynasty of the South and the North had close ties, they felt that now was the time to fight the Dynasty of the South; now that the Creator, they thought, had deliberately wiped out their ally. They were to expand their land to the North and the South possessing all the resources that they lacked. They calculated the costs, time, and types of machinery to be invented to carry out the plan and build mega structures. Plans were devised into how they were going to rebuild the new land. New names were devised and areas divided up more and more with leaders assigned to each area. Methods were devised for punishing law breakers and new rules were set.

In order to practice what the system will be once the Dynasty of the South has been conquered. The two Dynasties liaised in bringing offenders to justice by punishment, both young and old. Those in charge desperate to impress the higher authority were quick to condemn and punish offenders. The mood changed amongst the two Dynasties, discontent with the punishment imposed by fellow Dynasty.

This began the cultural change within the Dynasty. Before, cultural-differences were celebrated and were something of intrigue; it then became a major element of disgust and a tool for punishing those that were perceived as different. This was exacerbated between the East and the West Dynasties. Some of the annoyed and frustrated Dynasties from the West often shout:

"Go back to your land."

"You have destroyed yours, don't destroy ours; with your heavy footprints and oversized bodies."

Some also questioned why those from the East stayed in the best part of the settlement and were so kindly treated. The relocation to the West affected the Dynasty of the East severely, for it was a new climate and condition to adapt to. In addition, they were not getting the hibernation period, which over time weakened them. Change also affected their food.

As they were huge herbivores, due mainly because of the annual migration of wilder-beasts crossing from the dry south to the north of the land; they always had meat in plenty. In addition, the Dynasty of the North also used to reward them for works with meat. However, since the Tiron-tamada, this was no longer possible; such luxuries were a thing of the past. Their outstanding powers were now mere memory; rest and sleep they later realised was part of their source of power.

The commitment to their plan and growth, heated by their pride made them unable to reach out and ask for assistance from the Dynasty of the South; instead they traded with them. Blinded by their ego, they failed to realise that the more they afflicted fellow Dynasties, the hasher their conditions became. Also, the Creator had taken this understanding from them and some eminent scholars amongst them had lost their mind trying to find the cause, some even questioned the root of the Creator.

They thought about the problem philosophically, extolling their wisdom on how this had happened, rather than the reasons why it had occurred. It had now become their culture that anyone and anybody can be penalised and punished. Conditions became more hostile where brothers were killing each other and children plotting against their parents.

In the dream I saw how fellow Dynasties treated each other, and was shocked the people can be so wicked. The devices and tools they were using to detain those that had been found to be at fault were gut-wrenching. In the dream I saw a fellow Dynasty of the East angered by all this, ran into the crowd to save some of those held captive, but he himself was caught and detained by the incarcerators.

With less and less resources, all found thing difficult. Some members of the Dynasty from the West complained that they should not have to support those beasts from the East. That they consume on average, five times of the amount of food of the people of the West. In the heat of frustration, they shouted in accord:

'They eat like Gorillas and their behaviour is not that much better than wilder-beasts.'

However, putting their differences aside, they planned to combine forces and bring down the Dynasty of the South - the physical strength of the Dynasty of the East with the ingenuity, and expert knowledge of the Dynasty of the West.'

'I woke up in a state of shock disturbed by what I had seen. Well I tried to wake up but hunger gave me no strength. To wake, and walk was too much of a challenge, to move just my arm then would have been more than a great act; so I rested and saw more.'

Chapter Nine

CREATOR'S REVOLT

I looked on as Safarai remained in the closet of silence, so I continued. The Dynasties saw the Dynasty of the South as slow and always residing to fate. Moreover, they have never seen them create anything that the Dynasties would fear. In their assembly, one of the scholars stood up, and shouted:

'The South are not for war, in fact, they fear it. They are not able nor have the intelligence to prepare for battle; it is simply not in their nature.'

However, the Dynasty of the South were aware of the plans against them, and they too prepared, an entity that neither the Dynasty of the East or the West took into consideration. For they were too wrapped-up in their premature celebration of victory; confident of their mastermind. In their hunt for self-importance and domination, blinded by their greed and self justification, they ignored the Single rule - HARM NOT ONE ANOTHER - and put their interests first.

The Dynasties thought themselves wise by creating more rules as they themselves felt that the introduction of new laws would not be welcomed, but were adamant that the new rules must be imposed. In their argument, they stated that the Single rule one sided and did not cover all areas of life. Moreover, it was but a Single rule and there are many areas in a typical Dynasties daily practice. The rule they commented was also one-sided because it only protected the Dynasties and did not extend to the beasts of the field, the birds of the high sea and the mammals in the blue sea; some of which they felt were even better than some Dynasties.

'People,' they stated, 'are arrogant, difficult to control and undisciplined.' At least with animals they stated, 'their jour-neys are known, their patterns can be predicted and numbers counted. People on the other hand are very much different, troublesome lot they are,' said the elected speaker. The fad-ing tone of his words was warmly greeted with thunderous applause.

As a result, those not willing to adhere to the new laws

were humiliated in the market places and the open cage became their shelter. Young and old, male and female were left
outside in the heat of the high light during the day and the
cold at night. The rain, the grainy sea and many more they
endured. The offenders were placed in the middle of each Dynasties settlement so that all other Dynasties witnessed them.
It served as a warning and reminder to the rest of them. Daily,
they were taken to project sites for digging and carrying heavy
load to build projects of colossal scale and magnitude. The
rebuilding programme devised grinded to a halt. The Dynasty
of the East that were usually full of vigour, energy and en-
durance had lost their gifts. Now, working through the whole
year, the chemistry of their body and mind changed and large
numbers fell to minor ailment, larger numbers died.

'Night fell and the Dynasty of the West and the East set off on
their attack. As they drew nearer, still there was no sign of
the Dynasties of South's defences, victory unparalleled was
to be theirs. Then, the men, and women of the South started
raising the alarm, and the rest of the Dynasty joined. As the

advancing Dynasties approached, they could hear noises, the closer they got the more unbearable it became. The Dynasty of South played their instrument at all frequencies, and the sounds that coloured the air were deafening.'

'All the wilder-beasts the Dynasties brought for battle became disorientated, and running off course. Soon the riders themselves could not bear the noise. The noise moved from the sole of their feet to the top of their head. It shook their internal organs, and separated the blood from the water in their veins. It caused the connections, and ties they used to fall apart.

Beasts and other earth-burrowers dug up the path the Dynasties were to use. The earth was tilled as a farmer would. The ground was made to get worse and uneven so that whoever entered could not turn back. In some places, the dig was over ten times the height of a person. Much commotion filled the air; the grainy sea trembled as it swallowed all up. The land shook, and rivers and lakes burst their banks. The hot flowing river poured endlessly. Mountains and trees shattered. Now the persecutors and the persecuted were at the mercy of torment.'

'Now, all scrambled for survival. No one or thing was

safe. Soon, everyone realised that a higher force had been disturbed, and trembled with the catastrophe that was going to hit them. There were waves after waves of attacks on land and on the blue sea; both people and all creatures were to suffer. The very earth came alive, it roared like an over-sized wilderbeast, and its gritty saliva drooled for the blood of life. The grainy sea flooded the paradise, and snow descended with a ferocity and quantity never before witnessed. This was going to be the most catastrophic event the Dynasties have ever had to face where all will perish.'

'The Creator showed his affliction onto all living things, all at the same time. All was shattered. The air was filled with thick dust, and day became a stranger to night. Smoke, ice, the grainy sea and the blue sea interchanged, as they all competed for destructive dominance. Every valley was filled, and every ditch covered. The once colourful land changed to a monotonous, gloomy place. The high light moved closer, and the land felt like the heart of the hot river. Wind, the strongest of its kind, gathered strength and thundered past; it took all that was on its path. Darkness fell, and the land was un-inhabitable, even for the toughest beasts.'

'The blue sea and its wave rose in anger, higher than

the tallest mountain. It only departed after it had washed away the toughest hills and the established trees, even the Sube. The Creator opened the high sea and the land froze. All had nowhere to hide, and no living being will survive.'

'The Creator sent seven multi-headed fire that ravaged the land seven times. Hot river of unprecedented manner poured, and all were in chaos. Noise, panic, and apprehension ran riot through the whole land. The land was shattered into many pieces, and all perished. This was the reward for self-willingness to destroy, and misuse the powers bestowed to the people. The day was documented as one that the Creator demonstrated his anger to his creations and it was engrafted for eternity.'

'All tried to escape the terror but without success, all efforts resulted in vain. From that day onwards, the Creator decided not give any humankind such great powers that they once possessed, for they will only use it against their own kind and his creations.'

'The land that was above the sea became submerged and those below rose; the grainy sea was scattered across the blue sea. The event was called the Shunku-shunku-Gira-ma-satim muruli, meaning, the beginning and the end when the

Creator made anew all living things.

Chapter Ten

MIRROR

'**Well, that was an accurate description of what happened,**' commented Safarai, then he asked me:

Who told you all this?'

'No one, I saw it all in a dream', I replied.

'Dream, you mean no one told you?', he said.
'Come to think about it,' he said, like he just realised something, 'no one could have told you'. 'So where were you at the event and how did you survive?'

He continued to ask as if whatever I said was going to

change anything. So I replied:

'Like I said, I saw it all in a dream'.

'My son, why did you not tell anyone, why did you not consult the elders or at least let someone know?'

Then he paused as if he had said something wrong and said:

'You mean you were shown the event before it happened? But why, why you of all people, why did you not tell anyone?' he said as he was getting more irritated.

'That is what I have been trying to tell you all this time, but you were consumed in your "Valley of Isalamata," and how I "afflict your very soul"', I said.

'That was so senseless,' he replied.

'Oh, you stupid imbecile', said a voice out of nowhere. *'Why is youth wasted on the young and wisdom is en-*

dowed to those with dim wits? You are worse that the Mad prophet. You see again, everything you do, everyone you know, someway, somehow always do bad . . .'

'Failure, shut up, this is not the time for this' said Safarai in a sharp voice.

'Oh yes it is, it is the perfect time for it' he replied. 'What else are you planning to destroy? What I ask, are you conjuring up in your dark minds . . .'

'I did say that I was sorry,' I said to Failure as tears began to cloud my eyes. 'I just... I was making my way to tell anyone that I could find, but met no-one until I fainted and Safarai found me . . .'

'Fainted' replied Failure, 'you should have died with the rest of them you rascal. It will be you wouldn't it, Prophet-gone-bad that rescues the worthless; it will be you wouldn't it that either kills the innocent or saves the damned.'
'What use are you to anyone here along with your master of disaster? I heard you saying earlier how you hid

in the bush and refused help from your saviours. So, this was your plan all along, sitting on the secrets giving to you by the Creator. Now I have seen it all. '

'I thought that I had met the master polluter, the chief destructor, and the most with the worst ambitions; little did I know that Safarai was pale in comparison to you. At least he kills the innocent one at a time, he murders the helpless, and takes life to fulfil his own selfish endeavours. However, you manage to destroy the existence of all living life forms all because what, you were hungry and tired.'

'Who knows if you had only manage just to tell someone, somebody, somehow, somewhere; night and day will still exist, the night light and high light will still celebrate their dominance.'

'You. . . selfish, evil creature. I hope you feel much better now that your belly is full, and slumber has cleared from your eyes.'

Unprovoked, he continued his verbal assault against me and said:

'What worth is it now that you have strength but there

is nothing to fight for? What is the use of having a voice when there is no one to listen? What worth is your regret when there is none to compensate? Why bother now tidy your abode when there is no one to visit?'

I was about to speak when he continued again.

'So Safarai, now that we are all here, and baring out our souls, would you please explain why you were mating with a tree?'

'What do you mean?'

'What do I mean? You half-wit. Do you think that I did not see you? Naked and hugging the tree? How are you going to explain that, you disgusting waste of life? How can you create life with that which is not living? What indeed were you hoping to achieve?'
'So you cannot find yourself a woman from the plenty that were in your Dynasty. I remembered when you got really friendly with that Giselle, wanting her for a wife did you? You revolting monster. I have seen many people here on the

grainy sea, but you are something Safarai or should I say, you are something else.'

'The wilder-beasts know their boundaries, the Dynasties, even as backward as they are, know the difference between right and wrong sometimes; even the bird of the high sea knows its place and species. But you... Why, I ask you again, do you still breathe? Why is it that you still walk? Everyday, I wish that your life is shorter than each breath you take. I revel in the great anticipation that it will be your last; anger grips me again as your nostrils flutter to gather more air . . .'

'Failure . . .'

'Do not failure me, it is you that is the failure here. Even failure is too much of a good word for you because it involves a reward of meeting you at the end of it - what a waste of an effort. It would have been best if life just passed you by, better yet, if the wilder-beasts excrements take your place. At least in a little while, new shoots and life will follow.'

'You are one thing that the Creator should not have

created. *Your very presence enrages me. Each time we meet, my very spirit churns, and turns bitter. There is a reason for the wind, even the rotten leaf has a purpose. In all the years I have known you, none of them have been good . . .'*

'But surely the day I was born was good, the Creator does not just create, he does it for a reason, for a purpose . . .'

'Well I know your purpose, and I know your reason. The life should have been taken from you as soon as your mother was ready to conceive. Then we would have all been happy, and would have said that the Creator knew that this one was not worth it . . .'

'Now I see why you are the way you are, and why happiness and joy has been taken away from you. You think you know it all, but wisdom, and understanding is as far from you as the East is from the West . . .'

'What would you know about understanding? and do you not have wisdom as plenty as you do companions - none

existence. You are a failed fraudster. You could not even get your apprentice to talk to you normally; you had to resort to the Smoke of Truth. I saw you adding your potions to the fire to make him talk, or should I say, to make him tell you the truth. Is that not right Safarai, your secrets are safe with me, you evil Herbalist . . .'

'What is it that I have done to you that your love of hate for me is unfading, and it is forever strong?'

'You idiot, you and I will never see eye to eye. You are alive, that is why I hate you . . .'

'I indeed feel sorry for you . . .'

'You . . . sorry; what? I am sorry for everyone that knows you. I wish I did not know you, I wish nobody knew you. Safarai, I plea, just tell me, when is it that you will take your last breath?'

'Will you then leave me alone?'

'*Possibly not, but one thing is for certain, I will be following you even to your grave, and the life after that. You deserve no peace, you will get no peace, peace will not find you, ever . . .*'

'Then this exposes your folly. Whether I am breathing or not it makes no difference to you. Whether I am alive or not, you will still continue your barrage of disgust towards me. Is it not a shame that you have no life? Disappointing I know that you cannot live by yourself. Instead, you feed on my life to sustain yours, and whatever I do in your eyes is always wrong . . .'

'Is that all that you came up with, your foul intelligence insults me. Ha haa, please stop drowning me in your words of sewage . . .'

'It is your presence that is revolting, and every word that runs from your mouth forever dissolves my intestines. You said earlier that I was mating with a tree, which was not true. Do you know which tree I was hugging and the reason why?'

'Am I supposed to answer that or believe your fiction? I cannot believe that you opened your sewer trap, and just asked me that. Well, only those with dignity knows the hurt of shame, and only those that are worthy care what others thinks of them, neither of these are indeed related to you . . .'

'Talking sense to you is like looking for the grainy sea on the blue sea . . .'

'I will be an island on the blue sea, separate indeed from you and your foul works. Where I stand, I see the great expanse of your sorrow works. I wish that I were blind so that I do not have to see you; I wish I was lame so that I will not have to follow. I wish these ears of mine are deaf as not to hear you, I wish you were dumb so that I do not have to hear your voice. Shame be onto you Safarai, shame be onto all those that knows you, shame . . .'

'Enough', Takunta shouted to my relief. He then continued:

'Why condemn the innocent, and blame the one that it is not apportioned to? Were you not also warned of the Shunku-shunku? I ask, did the Creator not also spoke to you of the same event, but you also kept quite. Did you not dream dreams, and were you not shown visions? Well answer me and I will prove you wrong. You, and the rest of the Dynasties shivered in your shells, and asked, why am I the one been shown these dreams, why should I be the one to tell, and share my nightmares in the open. Have you forgotten that the Creator never does things without warning and, or without reasons?'

'Safarai were you, I ask, not also shown a similar dream many times over? Why then have you chosen to hand all the blame to one person, and hang all the mistakes on the young one's shoulders. The saving and warning of the Dynasties were in the hands of all. Everyone had the chance to change this outcome; all have the chance to change their fate. But all were weak; they all slumbered through the warnings.'

'Do not live with regrets nor dwell too long in the land of the dead. We have no power now, now that we are all but spirits, taking on many forms and shapes in the high sea. We have no powers now that our very bodies are buried with the others. The best we can all do now is wait in hope. Maybe someday, one day the Creator will give life to others to live again. If and when we get to see them, I hope that they will take heed, and listen to our voices, that they will take note, and act when the Creator speaks to them in dreams, and communicate with them in visions.'

The end of Takunta's speech was all a blur to me after he said that 'we are all but spirits, taking on many forms and shapes in the high sea', that our 'very bodies are buried with the others.'

'Bury . . . Dead . . . Spirits . . .'
These three simple words rang loud in my head over and over again. I grabbed Safarai, by the neck, and repeated the words to him again. He looked at me, smiled, and said 'welcome kid'.

'Welcome', I shouted, 'to where?' I asked with a jerky voice. I do not want to be dead . . . I am not dead . . . you all might be, but I . . . Am not. Tears gushed before I finished what I wanted to say. He looked at me and smiled again.

'But I am only eight years old,' I cried, 'I have not even lived yet; I do not even know what life is. Is the only memory of my existence going to be pain, suffering, and hardship? I mean . . . I . . . I did not chose for the Danda-maka-kojo's to destroy our Dynasty. Neither did I choose to live only to be teased, poked, and prodded continually by death. I did not choose to survive, to fall into the crevice and escape the jaws of the grim reaper only to land in into the angry jaw of pain. I was about to continue when Safarai, stopped me, and said:

'Son, you have fulfilled the purpose of your life, and the end of the living body has come.' 'Besides,' he said with a smile, 'you have just said "Danda-maka-kojo" without realising it.'

I paused and then said, 'no I did not, because that makes no sense. Why are you still making jest of me about the way I speak . . .'

'Son,' he said, '"Danda-maka-kojo" are terms in the language of the spirits, the Ngseuto, it means, "The Beasts of the Night."' He continued, 'the body might be

dead, but the Gira ploirante never dies.'

I said to him, 'so now it is your turn to be speaking "no sense and your wind blow with no direction," what is the Gira ploirante,' I asked in an angry voice.

He replied calmly, '"Gira ploirante" means the Breath of Life. These words are the language of the heavenly spirits, the language of those granted life when the body is no more. Only those granted the special grace can speak and hear it'

Chapter Eleven

REMEMBER

The King and the Queen,

The Prince and the Princess,

You remembered. . .

Chapter Twelve

MEMORIES

It was all the smoke, fire, tears, anguish, and everything else that just happened that calmed me. They made me remember a story my father once told. Well, I thought it was just a story, but wisdom has whispered to me that it was more than that; understanding opened the gates I had shut with my ignorance.

'Greetings.' He started.

'Let me welcome you to the Great Plains, the rocky ravines, and the most beautiful people in the world, where the wisest of minds dwell. Let us meet the greatest philosophers and mathematicians, the master scientists and alchemists; the land of creativity, of wonder, the land of amazement. Let

me introduce you to the greatest things, and greatest beings
that have ever lived.'

He continued:

'Come lose yourselves in the world of the prodigal
composers, and virtuoso musicians the world has ever seen.
Allow me to introduce you to the greatest wilder-beasts to
have ever roamed the land.'

'Long ago, there was a place at the deepest region of
the blue sea, and the highest point of the mountains, where
the hills and valleys; ridges, and plains of old are still in existence.

Let us take a journey to the Abyss, to the very dark,
very cold places; the forgotten world where life once thrived,
where secrets still lie. Here, the great mammoths venture not
to the upper layer of the blue sea nor feel the warmth of the
high light. Where the only source of brightness is those gen-
erated by the creatures themselves. Glowing light, twinkling
like stars, and with a sudden flash of lightening, the Abyss
is lit, revealing the vast underwater world, and its impressive
landscapes. Beasts here have become accustomed to the

dark. Here, darkness dominates.'

'Welcome to the place where fishes, and mammals of the blue sea break traditional rules like swimming backwards with incredible speed, and spiralling down, tail first, or flip from side to side as if being attacked by a savage, invincible predator. Some have eyes-lined backs, and others have skins tougher than rocks. Welcome to where it all began; enter the land of our ancestors.'

'Come and visit the places where these Dynasties lived. A place of varied colours, practices, gifts, and talents; where complex structures, abodes, and ingenuities reside. A place furnished with inventions of many kinds, where the people acquired wisdom, and document them in a variety of ways.'

'The weather was so dramatic that it changed the whole landscape. When the rain falls, it overturns the soil, mixed with the dispersed earth, stones, plants and debris. The river runs brown, gushing from the North to the South, giving strength to help it flow up, and over the Hills of Salandosa, the only place on the land where the water climbs up the mountain face.'

'Come,' he continued, 'and meet the four Dynasties

in the land, those of the North, the East, the South, and
the West.'

'The Dynasty to the North were tillers of the land.
They knew everything about making the land produce boun-
tiful harvests. They were astronomers, and knew precisely
when, and where rain will fall. The Dynasty to the East
were warriors; their men were the strongest in the land. The
Dynasty to the South were the first musicians, and made
melodies that was sweeter than honey. The Dynasty to the
West were the most attractive in the entire land, their sons
and daughters were adorable. Generations after generation,
they become more beautiful beyond measure. The clothes
they wore were made of the finest materials; their abodes
were crafted to also reflect their beauty.'

'The Dynasty to the North knew about time, and
what can be done in season. The most lavish colours
adorned their landscapes. Fruits, and vegetables of every
kind was abundant; their homes, and fields were filled with
sweet scents. They had intricate knowledge of all things
relating to the Land, including the high light, the wind, the
night light, the rain, and the stars. They enjoyed the cool

wind from the West, and the warm from the South.'

'They were short in stature and dressed to suit their job. They were literally, off the earth and were not shy of it. The colours they wore matched the powder earth, their abodes seemingly hued from it. All they wore on their feet, head, and around their waste seemed to have been kissed, and caressed by the powder earth. Most of their time was spent outdoors apart from during the raining season. Even then, they planted trees whose branches and leaves are high, and wide to protect the area of their settlement from heavy rain.'

'They lived deep in the jungle, surrounded by the lush savannah. Other Dynasties described their settlement as a paradise. The Dynasty of the South often made references to their settlement in their songs. The land is adored by the most beautiful flowers, birds, and mammals, with the brightness and boldest of colours. Whenever an animal is taken for meat, they pray to it so that its soul rests in peace, and thank it for giving up its life for extending theirs. Such was the intertwined relationship between The Dynasty of the North and the environment they lived in.'

'The Dynasty of the East were the mightiest of them all. They had no fear, and were decorated with unsurpassed strength. One man has the equivalent power of ten men of other Dynasties. They have very strong legs and arms, and were equipped with amazing speed. They tended not to work all day long. For work that would have taken other Dynasties one day to complete, took them a quarter of the time.'

'They were also the tallest, and heaviest of all the Dynasties, just like their abodes. Their structures were tall with huge supporting members. The largest tree trunks were used to construct their homes. They had devices for lifting, pushing, and pulling heavy materials such as stone across land and over hills. They were all like Kings; they feared nothing, and no-one. Beasts bowed in their presence, other Dynasties were in awe of their strength. Some believed if the Creator were to ever walk the land, he would be in the image of this Dynasty.'

'When they shouted forests shiver, when they run trees trembled from their roots. They climbed the highest tree, and swam the deepest rivers. No mountain was too high, no journey too far. Their children kept wild-beasts as pets, and the parents wrestle Apes for sport. Brute force they have in plenty with astonishing hunting abilities. They have numerous and complex ways of setting traps and preserving their meat when these become scarce. The Dynasty do not hunt during their hibernation period where none of them can be seen, as they enter deep into the belly of the land.'

'They crumbled rocks with their bare hands, and wrestle the biggest Gorillas. They no longer competed against themselves but used animals and nature for determination. Each year they hosted a contest called the Seven Pillars of Strength. The first challenge was a swim against Dolphins, the second, a race against a Cheater, the third, wrestling with a Gorilla, fourth, tree climbing against a Monkey, fifth, log throwing against a Mammoth, sixth, race against the wild horses of Pashan, and the seventh test was a combination of all of these, catching the Choord bird.'

Frightened and amazed at the same time with all he had said so far, I asked him at the time what a Choord bird was? I know my father, he can wrap the most mundane things in his blanket of illuminating words, and make it seem like something else. I wished I had his gift. The Choord bird is probably a small bird that feeds on tiny worms, I said to my-self at the time.

Like he was reading my thoughts, he walked over and sat next to me. Whispering, and sometimes shouting dramati-cally, his face lit up as if he was standing face to face with the bird. He made many gestures of the bird, and tried it seemed, to convince me of its existence, then he continued:

'The Choord bird is the mystical bird that not only does it have speed, and strength in abundance it is also bless-ed with the gift of vanishing. Whilst its colours, textures, and size are overwhelming; its movement, and poise are equally mesmerising. Like water, it can be as light as air, and then, it can be as stern as a rock. Whilst it can be as small as an ant, it can be bigger than the largest mammal in the sea. With its multitude of gifts, it confuses the most agile feet, and knots the most capable minds. Those that compete against the Choord often lose because of the bird's hypnotic display of transfiguration, and its unexpected actions rather than its strength. Indeed, the Choord is one of the entities that linked the four Dynasties.'

'Its claws are toughened by fire, and cooled by the

ice, this gave it the toughest claws known to the Dynasties, if not the toughest, and hardest thing ever created. For it is like a living rock, and is the sharpest thing known in the land. It has cavities in its body where ice and the hot river run. It can keep itself warm when it is bitterly cold and cool when it is hot. It has a span over the height of twelve people, and can drink a lake dry.'

As he continued, I imagined the bird in its full splendour, its majestic colours, spreading those long, sweeping wings, and hovering over us as the story continued, as if to prove its existence. He continued:

'Its beak, skull, and claws are tougher than the hardest rock, for they have been heated, and cooled by the furnace, a process that is Millennia's old. How did the Dynasties know this? In one of its battle, the Choord bird chipped one of its claws in Mount Sumbiti, and was discovered by the Dynasty of the West whom since the incident had been developing a materials similar to it.'

'The bird, though being the biggest birds in the land, it is lighter than air, and can take on many forms, shapes, and guises at will due in part to its interlocking, and multi-hinged skeleton. This makes it virtually impossible to trap, let alone kill. How can you fight an enemy that you cannot see? How can you deliver a blow to that which you cannot feel? How can you drown the one that dwells in the deepest sea? How can you flatten that which has no thickness, and can fly through mountains? How can you suffocate one that needs no air? Well, it goes back to the Rameta bird', he exclaimed.

I was intrigued because of all the stories he had told me; he has never mention something as dramatic as this to me. At the time, I said well, he does love an audience. I listened as he continued:

'The Rameta bird became the Choord bird but before this, it was the most disliked creature of all things. It was hated by all the people and was caste-aside by fellow birds. The wilder-beasts charge it when they see it, and the mammals of the blue sea splash water to display their disgust. It was a scavenger, and it was not in its nature for cleanliness. It reeked.'

'Rameta birds always seem to hobble, and hop around

because one of their legs is longer than the other. They had septic moles on their faces, and neither were their wings equal; they were flightless birds. Until one day, one of the Rameta birds, seeing the way others treat its species confided in the Creator. In its anger he shouted:'

"Oh Creator, why make our species a generation of flightless birds, I have never seen a fish that cannot swim. Even if only one of us is saved of all the species, then grant it."

'In tears he continued:'

"Let the chosen one be the most powerful, and be the greatest of all birds." 'He asked the Creator to combine all existing Rametas into one, and for it to be gifted beyond comprehension in return for its handiwork. He wanted the Creator to give the chosen one a task that will benefit all creations, where it will be the most celebrated and appreciated in all the land; for it to be the greatest living thing ever created, and that will always live. The Rameta bird that was saying all this was Kea-nibu.'

'To change the condition of its species, he started walking from the settlement of the Dynasty of the North then to the West, the South, and East over, and over again, a reverse direction to the nature of things in the land. He walked around all the settlements continually for a total of seven years, pleading with the Creator; day after day, night after night, season after season. He continued in the rain, in the high light, in the snow, on the plains and over the mountains. He walked the arid desert, through the troubled waters and the deepest valley, knowing not that year after year, the Creator was changing him to fulfil his requests.'

'Although transformation was happening, he did not realise it. His tears, laced with sorrow, had made its eyesight improve ten folds. Over time, the hanging warts on his face, and legs had disappeared, and the years of exposure to the harshness of environment had cured its foul stench which encouraged its feathers to grow longer, lighter and more powerful.'

'The time spent walking in the wilderness had helped Kea-nibu learn from things around him. The way the wind blows, its force, frequency, and temperature. He had learnt how the grainy sea shifts and creates its shapes, and colours. He knew the journeys each grain engaged in.'

'He had listened to the rustling trees, the swaying of the long grass, and saw the many different colours, and textures of flowers of the field, and of the wild. He had heard, and committed to memory the loud noise of the waterfall and the quietness of the night. In patience, he had watched time stood still, and had understood the nature of the shimmering forms of the blue sea, the gentleness of the waters and the unparalleled powers of the waves.'

'Kea-nibu had looked up as far as the eyes can see, and saw the deepest of dungeons, and meditated on the greatness of the Most High. He had walked the on the powder earth when it was at its coldest, and trampled it at its hottest.'

'The day came when Kea-nibu was going to be transformed. He was walking along the arid desert, suddenly, everything stopped. The wind stopped blowing, the noise retreated to its source, the grainy sea stopped moving, the blue sea and rivers halted their movements. Time itself feared leaning forward.'

'Then, the ground that he stood on turned into ice. To the right of him it was day, and the left, night. Next, a ring of fire formed around him. The fire was as high as the mountain of Sube and its width was twenty times the span of the tallest person. The living fire swirled to, and thro, inside was Kea-nibu being thrown around violently.'

'Scared, and unsettled, he screamed in anguish, frightened at what was happening. This he concluded was because he was being punished for all he had been saying to the Creator. The sight has never been witnessed before nor ever since. All stopped, and saw the spectacle, and thought that the end had come.'

'The sounds that filled the air was like the rushing of many waterfalls; the land shook to its core as all witnessed the re-birth of the Rameta bird becoming the Choord bird. The event lasted from when the high light was at its highest to its setting. The day was called the Humbat-imu-Rameta, meaning, the Spiritual renewal of the Rameta bird.'

'As it had dramatically appeared, the fire disappeared again, leaving behind piles of ashes. Underneath the charred earth was the Choord bird that could not be seen for another ten days, it laid on the same spot for a further seven. Since then, no other living thing has possessed the great diversity of his talents, strength, and ability.'

'The Choord bird became important to the Dynasties because they can make patterns on the ground either by drawing on it or using twigs, stones, mounds of earth, and so on to convey information. It was believed that they taught the first people how to communicate in the written form. The Choord bird was the only one from all the animal kingdom given an unequivocal immunity from harm. A rule that was respected by all the Dynasties not only for the knowledge it had imparted but also for the mystical power it possessed. The Choord bird is the only creature that has met the Creator face to face, but its senses were paralysed so not to be able to describe the Creator.'

'The Choord bird dwells in the land of the Dynasty to the West where the freezing snow meets the hot running river. Due to its works, patches of the land can be in full blossom when other areas are covered in snow. Therefore, the Creator used the Choord bird to carry out the requests of the people, even if they may be out of season.'

After the description of the Choord bird, he went to describe the other two Dynasties, the Dynasty of the South and the Dynasty of the West. He said:

'The Dynasty of the South were music makers, and

had uncountable numbers of instruments. They had amazing singing voices with incredible vocal ranges. They could hold a note at the same pitch until the high light sets; with their songs, they could melt the most-stubborn of hearts. They were capable of demolishing mountains, and communicate with all beings and creatures. They could use their drums to summon help from the Dynasty of the West or send warning to the Dynasty of the North. Their senses were so acute that they could hear a butterfly flap its wings from a long distance. Their knowledge of the natural environment around them was so that they communicated with mammals of the sea to the smallest insect on a branch of a tree.. It is once believed that during a harsh long drought, they made joyful sounds that the sky opened and poured forth rain'

'The Dynasty of the South were the first group that was formed. They grew in numbers and decided to start settling in other places of the land. As a result, their second place of settlement was to the North, the third was to the East, and the fourth, to the West. Whilst each Dynasty knew their particular land, and all that surrounded it, The Dynasty of the South knew all the land, and its settlement. They were the first to develop writing, painting, construct abodes and the first tools of any kind.'

'They documented the land, illustrating the hills and rivers, the Great Plains, the powder earth and the blue sea, tree, rocks, valleys, and ridges and all that lived there. They recorded how long it takes to travel to places, how far places were. They knew the species of animals that resided in particular places, their migration patterns, and numbers. They knew all the different forces and types of wind. They have names for different flows of streams and rivers. They were the best medicine people, using the herbs, leaves, and trees of the land to cure all manner of illness and sickness.'

'They were influenced by animals around them and made their homes on the mainland. Sometimes mimicking what they see around them and other time building high over the ground to survey the landscape; uttering sounds, from the highest point to communicate to the birds in the high sea, calling out to mammals in the sea.'

'They could be on the ground making music, stumping their feet, hitting the powder earth with instrument to speak to animals that dwell deep in the ocean. When all this is combined, the whole settlement becomes a heaving, buzzing, and lively place. Music was in their very nature. They believed that sound never dies, that sounds are sacred. Therefore, the Dynasty were very conscious of the sounds they uttered particularly those for good fortunes.'

'They had a refined acute sense of hearing, and can feel, and hear vibrations other Dynasties could not. Throughout their existence, they had developed musical instruments, and talents beyond comprehension. The biggest is the Imprado, a 10-person piece of instrument that is carved out of a log. The other versions are circular in form and they spend over a year, curing, carving, tuning and preparing the Farmasa. When these are placed together and they perform, the music is simply breath taking. These are arranged to create the best quality of sound.'

'It is believed that even today when you see trees waving from side to side and making rustling sounds, they are dancing to the music the Dynasty of the South that was created all those times ago. Similarly, when people say that they heard a piece of music in their sleep; it is the sounds that the Dynasty of the South uttered all those millennia's ago. Sounds, as they believed, never die.' They believe that seasons may come and go; people may change from generation to generation, but sound is always created, noise is ever-present. Every step that is taken makes a sound. Every breath from the nostril, every clap of the hand, every stomp of the feet, every beating of the wing, every motion of the heart; fire makes sounds, even the flickering flame is never silent.'

'Now, for the Dynasty of South's abode. Welcome to the open plains. The only place amongst the Dynasties where you can look as far as the eye can see and there are no hills or mountains. A land where even trees hardly touch the ground like it is some kind of a sacred place. Where the populace resided upon high with their strong believe that the closer one is to the high sea, the closer one is to the Creator. They also developed techniques of travelling up, and down the great heights, and have developed the most advanced method of living at the tree-top with intricate network of high sea walkways, and connecting ladders. They have amazing balance of the feet, and the most acute of hearing. They can mimic the howling wind, the thundering earth, and the rainfall. They watched the wilder-beast's movements, the shimmering of the blue sea, and the high light, and turned them into music. They are the only Dynasty that could hear undetectable sounds and play it.'

'They associated with the birds, and in turn, they of-fered them protection. But only one kind of tree was used for the abode, the Sube tree. It grew as high as mountains and its branches out only at the top; its form was slender, and strong. On some cloudy days, their tops cannot be seen; they   mysteriously disappear into the heavens. The Sube also had another purpose. When the great flood of Ne-fe-hea came, it swept all that was in its path, only the Sube remained after its wake.'

'The best spectacle however was when they put on a show, the land buzzes with excitement. Trees sway to the rhythm, new plants hop, rivers rumble, and swirl, and the grainy sea transfigures to show their appreciation.'

'They orchestrate the whole event beautifully. Start-ing organically with each member of the Dynasty seemingly seating in random places; playing unsynchronised sounds. Gradually, other members join in. Another beat, another sound, another dance, another vocal; soon the Plains is filled with the richest sounds; heaven, some believed, must be like this. Most of their time is spent playing musical instruments; finding another way to play a tune; another way to project

the vocals. Listening, looking, learning, and etching their lyr-
ics on tree barks, deep carvings on the trunks following a circular, spiral form. Even now that the original Dynasties are
no longer around, their work can still be heard as the wind,
and rain caresses the tree, giving back to nature what the
Creator had given to them.'

'Every tone they uttered, and beat stroked they
believed are not lost into the air, and forgotten. They are
absorbed into the powder earth, the blue sea, and all that
surrounds. Whilst the high light, and the night light have its
seasons, and the rain, and storms gather, and go; sound
they believed is everlasting. Sound created, they believed,
always comes back to the source that created it.'

'They adored their face, their hands, fingers, legs, and
hair with different patterns and colours. Those that were
the most decorated were the Poko Dynasty. It is said that
before the trees grew as tall as they were, they were the first
Dynasty of the powder earth and they adored themselves in
these ways to camouflage both their physical presence and
their natural body scent.'

'The ancient belief was that in the face of danger you either
run or fight. The Poko's were wiser than this. If generation

after generation you have learnt that neither of these tac-
tics work, then you need to find other means. They believed
that you are better off staying where you are, conserve your
energy, and transfer it to Zumete energy, that is, stillness.
Once they are in this state, not even the most astute sense
of any beasts, birds, and mammals of the sea senses, see or
smell them.

The texture, and colour of their skin become like the tree,
the rock or the grass they are adjacent to. As a result, they
developed complex patterns that could not be detected by
the sharpest eye. Indeed, they could suddenly turn into a living forest, mimicking sounds they know frightens the deadli-
est predator; terrifying the one that brings terror, outwitting
the wisest killer.'

'This was the greatest survival skill ever possessed by
any Dynasty. Through their observations, they had learnt
the sounds to communicate with all the Creator's beings.
But likewise, they used the technique for ambushing preys
too. Consequently, on a general day to day basis, some
members of the Dynasty wear leaves, barks, and branches
from different trees around their heads and waists. They
wear even more prior to the great hunt where no one could

tell the difference between them, and their surroundings.'

'The Dynasty of the West was the most adored and most beautiful, not only this, they were also great philosophers and thinkers. They were master crafts men and women and could turn an ordinary stone into the most adored object. They live in two types of abode, those formed out of rock and those from ice. Precious, beautiful stones were discovered particularly in the Hills of Stalia; stones that were truly amazing. Some were as clear as water, some were frosty, others were earth-coloured, and some shone like the midday high light. They adorned themselves, their clothes and abodes with stones of different hues, for they believed that stone was the toughest mineral ever created. They produce ornaments in ice and then treat them so they last for longer. One of them was presented to The Dynasty of the South, all gathered and watched as the sculpture slowly transformed, glittering and melting in the high light. The beauty they said is that ice sculptures are temporary; it also challenges them to create, invent and make new ones. In their homes, the floors are finished with stone and channels of the hot river runs underneath them and kept them warm. The hot flowing river is also conducted throughout the whole settlement in a variety of ways.'

'Water and stones were valued immensely by the Dynasty. Consequently, they devised machines to carry-out tasks for digging, purifying, washing, and shaping them. They had pulleys, moving parts, weights for loading, and unloading, and mechanisms that pushed, pulled, and pumped. Each year they hold an exhibition and demonstration the latest devices.

The arena is always full of astonishing inventions never before seen in the land. They invite other Dynasties to the event to show their latest inventions, but more importantly to reach out to fellow Dynasties and express their kinship and affirmation. The invitees are treated with the most dignity and are furnished with gifts of ointments, and precious stones. It was a time for celebration, and relaxation, where the Dynasties exchange stories, and general camaraderie.'

'The Dynasty of the West are gifted in manufacturing and trade. And found other means of exchanging for the materials, goods, and resources they lacked. They developed machinery to predict the weather and lift loads that even The Dynasty of the East could not carry.'

Chapter Thirteen

Rebound

It is only now that it is all making sense. Time and the insights of Safarai and Takunta have helped me stitched together the myriad shattered pieces of my thoughts. Fury and mistakes are never far from each other, whereas life and death will never dwell in a being at the same time. Wisdom often comes after we have wallowed in folly; despair though brief can last a lifetime. Many opportunities present themselves in life for us to make a change, many chances offer themselves to us to change our fate.

It is only now that I realise that the present uses the past to make a better future. Out of all these three elements, the past is the strongest of them all; for we are trying to either recreate it or avoid it. The present is volatile, and the future is known only because it is an understudy of the past.

I am Nzé, born to the Dynasty of the North. My father's name was Izžu, from the Dynasty of the South; my mother, Zaphinine, from the Dynasty of the West. After the famous battle of Libli, where my father defeated the Choord bird, his reward was to choose anything that he wanted on the grainy sea. Some elders thought he might choose to be the ruler of all the Dynast, others thought he might form his own settlement, instead, he chose my mother. Surely that is not such a great prize you might say, but the circumstances that surrounded this was anything but normal.'

'Many years before I was born, every seven years, a group of young people is sent on a journey of learning, of development; more importantly, a journey to ensure the survival of all of the Dynast. Four young people are chosen from each Dynasty and eight elders, both male, and females are chosen to give an in-depth explanation of their Dynasty as well as others. A year is spent in each Dynasties settlement starting in the South before they move to the West, North and so on.

Each Dynasty, although exposed to, and has knowledge

of the attribute about the other Dynasties, however, they can never be equal, let alone surpass the other Dynasties in their particular gift. Therefore, no one from the Dynasty was ever stronger than those from the Dynasty of the East. No-one is ever more beautiful than those from the West. The Dynasty of the South was simply better at playing, and composing music, none can surpass the Dynasty of the North in astronomy.

Well, all that was about to change. A child born in the Dynasty of the South was quiet exceptional. He seems to have developed the characteristics, and talents of each Dynasty. He had an acute sense of hearing, knowledge of nature, and the animals that dwell therein. His amazing strength, his speed on open ground, and his artistry with stone, earth, and timber surpassed those of the East and West Dynasties. He understood the complex laws of astronomy and was endowed with abstract thoughts and patience. He sang like another being with his melodious and storytelling qualities; he was a warrior that had no fear.

The day arrived when the pilgrims were to be tested on the land to the East at the end of their stay. He was the last person to take part and was the last day of the tournament.

All other six tests of the Pillars of Strength went well for him as expected but the last event, catching the Choord bird was to be a formality where the participants fail no matter how valiant their efforts. That day my father had made up his mind that this was not going to be his fate.

'As soon as the sixth event finished and he saw the Choord bird at a distance, he used the Zumete to make himself invisible and no-one could see him. The Choord bird, bounded to the perimeter of the arena, could not see him; neither could anyone else in the audience. In his Zumete state, he pleaded to the Creator to hold still the high light, there everyone stood including the Choord bird. He then pleaded again to the Creator to send rain only onto the area where the Choord bird was. The rain poured heavy and slowly but surely, the full scale and size of the bird started revealing itself. One of its wings was longer than the height of seven people and its body was bigger than an elder male from the Dynasty of the East. One its eye was the size of a person's head, and its claws were the size of a person.'

'The Choord bird was a magnificent bird, its feathers glimmer like the high light, and changed continually like the colours of the fruit of the Dynasty of the North. Unlike its overpowering appearance, its movement was gentle and graceful. He looked at my father, his head dwarfing him and he said, "Creator allowed."'

'Whilst the time was frozen, my father stood in front of it and looked at it. The Żumete energy ended and the crowd came back to their senses again. In front of them was rain that pours solely in a spot. As it waned, two figures stood in front of them at a distance. On the left was the Choord bird, and on the right, my father. They both stood facing each other, drenched by the heavy rain.'

'They stood for a while longer and the whole audience were amazed to silence. For none had seen the Choord bird at such a close proximity before. It wrote on the grainy sea in front of him, "Creator allowed", then it flew off, and disappeared into the high sea. My father stood unable to move, his spears and arrows laid on the floor next to him. Drenched, and breathing heavily, he looked as if he had just run to the land of the Dynasty of the North and back. He fell to the ground knee first and in tears.'

The crowd stunned momentarily, paused to take-in what they had just witnessed. Then, they cheered, ran out to him, and carried him on their shoulders, singing and shouting

his name. Amazed that such a young person can achieve such
a great feat. In the crowd was my mother who also witnessed
the occasion. It was later that day that he chose my mother to
be his wife.'

'Now for the great Zaphinine, my mother. Many years
before she met my father, she had a dream similar to the one
I had regarding the Single rule. She went and told the elders
but they did not believe her and said that they had more important things to do. Then one of them stood up and said:'

'"Well, if it is not our friend Zaphinine again. Back are
you to scare us all again with your lies? Was it not you that
said the Rameta bird will become a very important bird to all
the Dynasties; that foul, disgusting bird, that cannot even fly.
Was it not you that said a great destruction will come to a Dynasty and evil beasts of streaming fire, and smoke will come,
and crunch their very bones? Remind us again about our son
that will be lost in the wilderness and will face great hardship.
Tell me if I am not correct Zaphinine, was it not you that was
here only the other day, telling us all about the bitter goblet of
blood. When will you stop all these hallucinations, is it when

it is beaten out of you?"'

'However, at the assembly of the elders when she was telling them about the dream was Hjoty, the Priestess. As she was leaving, she approached her and asked her whether or not what she was saying was the truth, which she confirmed. She then told her to meet her in her abode the following day. She got there and told her everything saying that she saw two great Dynasties fighting to their destruction. She explained the details to her of which she noted. After she had left, Hjoty consulted the oracles and asked whether any of her stories were true, and they confirmed that it was indeed.'

'Following that, she went to the Dynasty leaders and explained the dream to them again. But rather than taking the step to avoid the situation, they prepared for the battle instead. Seven days later the leaders called a meeting and invited other elders from the Dynasty of the East saying that the Dynasties need to prepare for battle, that an imminent threat was about to happen and all need to prepare.'

'At the gathering, my mother ran onto the arena and said that what the Dynasties were planning was wrong as it is against the rule of the Creator but the elders ignored her again and stated that:

'She did not understand the benefits that will result from the expansions. That the very resources the Dynasty of the South and of the North are sitting on, languishing upon, and for some reasons, preserving, is the very materials they needed to make life better - to build a better life for all the Dynasties. This, they justified, was a great opportunity to create a great plan, a masterplan that all the Dynasties in the land can, and will follow in millenniums to come. They reasoned that though there maybe some losses, but the benefits will far outweigh the cost of putting the operation to action.'

Consequently, she decided to approach the Dynasty of the South and tell them all that the two Dynasties were planning. That day, she decided to journey to the land of the South and managed to convince her elder brother Laminine to follow her on the trip. They left under the cover of darkness on the long journey through the hills, and valleys of the snow covered landscape. When they arrived, and she delivered her message, they too did not believe her initially, so she went about to prove that all she was saying was the truth. The Dynasty sent out the great flock of birds of Itoi to survey, and report the findings to them. The flock returned and confirmed as my mother had described.

The Dynasty of the South honoured her for her brevity, and care for the people, and the animal kingdom not only for the benefit of the Dynasty of the South, but for all in the land. The elders of the Dynasty of the South all got together and sent messages to the Dynasties of the East and West and later visited them. They then all agreed to stop the fighting and all attacks that were been meditated.

Takunta and Safarai explained all this to me. This helped me comes to terms with my inner self. They told me that I was actually in the wilderness for fourteen years, and not just one has I originally thought. Safarai smiled and said: 'I was going to tell you at the time. That was why I was surprised when you said that you were only eight years old.' It was then he said, that he decided that it would be better if 'I discovered myself by myself.'

I was told that I actually left my body when Safarai tried to save me, and in doing so he lost his earthly-body too.

Then I remembered what he said that he had 'no power to give or take life, only the Creator does.'

They also explained that the only reason I was able to hear and see Safarai's inner voice, Mystery, which he referred to as Failure, was because I had become a spirit in the high sea. The reason it had taken on a form of itself was that Safarai was a great person.

'Takunta's voice rang in my ears as I remembered what he said, that 'the greater our aspiration, the louder the inner voice becomes to stop us from achieving our goals'. That it does all its best in 'trying to stop us achieving our calling.' I also remembered him saying that: 'The greatest battle we all face is not out there, rather what is in here,', that is, our mind. Safarai, I thought had definitely won that battle.

'The Goddess of the Trees was probably what Mystery referred to when he said Safarai was mating with a tree. She is the Zumete energy because she forfeited her earthly-body form to become the Goddess.

When I was in my 'Chambers of dreams,' I was not dreaming at all. Rather, they were premonitions, visions, and prophetic images been given to me. Hunger, they explained to me, was actually a tool the Creator used to keep me alive, to keep me searching, to keep me going.'

Safarai's Ball of Wonder was where he kept all that he owned; all that he knew. When he said that I probably had an 'unfinished calling' to complete, he was right. The Fire of Confession and the Smoke of Truth got the words out of me. It would have been terrible for me to have carried the message to the other side without blessing them with my Gira ploirante. This is why when many leave the body; they cannot speak the Ngseuto, the language of the heavenly spirits.

Both Takunta and Safarai explained to me that once we leave the body, we go through the Seven changes of Life where we pass through that thing we feared the most whilst we were alive so that the body and the spirit can rest peacefully. The Abyss of Alvi that Safarai mention I was told was the last phase of my changes. I have always feared the blue sea, unlike my father of course.

The Single rule that was broken simply stated, Tola-mala-tin-ziba-kore, meaning, HARM NOT ONE ANOTHER. I guess Takunta was right when I first met him and said:

'Your kind complicates the simple, yet the simplest things escape them. We have no reason to divide the things that keep us whole.'

Why I asked myself, could we not have understood a simple, basic rule?

Chapter Fourteen

PREMUNITION

The strange voices in my head that always talks about "The King and the Queen" and 'Remember, remember . . .' was indeed my mother's.

After reciting all I remembered, they explained that the narrative was an allegory used to explaining our land, the Land of Nza, surrounded by the blue sea to children at an early age. Takunta said she was fulfilling her duty as a mother to tell me the history of our land as all mothers had done. He said this has been done from generation to generation because she lost you at an early age he said.

As he spoke, The Seer unwrapped his Ball of Wonder and took out a wood-carving with many ridges and jagged edges. He held it on his left palm and pointed as he explained and said:

> Remember the King and the Queen,
> And their throne that faces the West,
> Much trouble brews in their chests,
> Calamity is spread on their skin.

This first part of this refers to the land in that it outlines to the West. The settlement of the Dynasty of the West resembles the profile of a man, a King. The second profile parallel to the King's resembles a woman, his Queen. The second part relates to the destruction the Dynasties will plan in the heart-land of the settlement and the unrest that will follow as a result of it.

> The love,
> The strong love will soon be broken
> And tears will fill all

This relates to the bond between the Dynasties been

broken as a result of their actions and exploits, but in the end, it is they that shall suffer for it.

> *Where are their mighty men of battle?*
> *Where is their beautiful Princess?*
> *Surely one can save*
> *Surely all have the strength.*

This asks why is there no-one stopping the planned acts of violence. That surely, not all are blinded and are thinking alike. The last prose means that everybody has the power to stop the beckoning atrocity.

> *The Queen,*
> *Her bejeweled neckwear will be loosed*
> *Her precious stone; buried.*

This refers to the area to the South of Nza, alluded to as 'Her bejewelled neckwear'. The 'loosed' refers to the digging-up and breaking-up of the beautiful plains; whilst the 'precious stones' means life, that is, all living things. The word 'buried' means lives will be lost, 'buried' under the grainy sea.

The King,
His crown of glory will be taken,
His ruling staff broken,
Naked, he shall flee.

Here, 'glory' refers to lives which will be lost. The 'broken' 'staff' of the King relates to the end of rulership by those in power. The King fleeing 'naked' is the unexpected and unprecedented event that will happen to the land. The scale and size of the destruction are one never before witnessed, where all shall regret.

Remember the Prince and the Princess,
He with the watery eyes,
She with her green eyes and treasured pearls.

The 'Prince' and the 'Princess' referred to is the profile and outline of the land to the North and to the East of Nza. The Prince's 'watery eyes' refers to the Lake of Iskoyi. The reference to the Princess's 'green eyes' is the Oasis of the East, and the 'treasured pearls' is a reference to the Sube-mai trees.

> *Remember the King and the Queen,*
> *Remember the Prince and the Princess*
> *Remember, remember. . .*

This meant forget not the land of Nza, the valuable, precious land. Make all efforts to warn all the Dynasties.

> *Remember the strong couple of the land,*
> *The King with fire in his breath,*
> *And Ice on his eyes.*

'... the strong couple' refers to the male and female fertility of life, meaning the providers and carriers of life. References to the 'fire' and the 'ice' refer to the flowing hot river of

the Hills of Stalia, and the snow-capped mountain of Mount
Bila-Guro; relating to the Tribe of the West's settlement.

His voice has power,
It shakes and trembles all,
His words are hot and harsh,
But forgiving.

All this relates to the eruption of the hot flowing rivers that flows intermittently, situated in the West of Nza. The
word 'forgiving' refers to the intermittent flow of the hot flowing river, whilst also meaning that the 'harsh' environment has
nonetheless allowed the Dynasties to dwell near and around
it.

The King's words bring life,
They bring new life,
They never fail.

This refers to the river Rtenoi-Pyepe, flowing from the

West to the East, bringing 'new life', that is, water, to the inhabitants of Nza.

> Remember his Queen,
> Her heart is calm with peace,
> She flows gently,
> Like a river.

The references to 'heart,' 'calm,' 'peace', and 'flow' all refer to the Valley of Isalamata, a place of serenity where all the Tribes meet on occasions.

> They all gather in her bosom for knowledge,
> For her mind is beautiful,
> She is forever thinking of Paradise.

Gathering in her 'bosom' also refers to the Valley of Isalamata, the centre of learning and knowledge for all the Tribes. The latter prose 'thinking,' refers to the 'head' of the Queen, that is, the settlement of the Tribe of the North which all Dynasties call 'Paradise.'

Remember the King and the Queen,
They both breathe and speak life
But hurry,
For they may change their words.

The 'breathing' and 'speaking' of 'life' also refers to river Rutenoi-Pyepe. It confirms its importance as a life-source for all the inhabitants of Nza. The urgency referred to relates to the change in the flow of river Rutenoi-Pyepe. In the winter it dramatically changes direction and flows from East to West, rather than West to East at other times in the year.

Remember, remember. . .

This is a reminder not to forget to tell others in order to avoid the fate.

The King and the Queen,
The Prince and the Princess
You remembered. . .

This was to confirm that the advice had been followed as communicated.

Chapter Fifteen

OPTIMISM

Even though they said that I had fulfilled my unfinished task, one thing that I still cannot come to terms with is the loss of my father, and mother, and Jelë. As I said that I heard a voice coming from the grainy sea that sounded familiar.

Safarai, looked at me, smiled, and said 'oh yes,' there is one more thing . . . Jelë Gira ploirante, that is, Jelë is alive. She was the only survival, but because you are now here, she cannot see you or hear you.

I looked and cried as I saw her. Tears turned bitter in every corner of my mouth. I looked again, and listened as she spoke . . .

Where now is my light?

Now that my inner shine has been dimmed,

The outer put out.

The night of the great noise,

Of the terrifying beasts,

I looked, and screamed for you,

But you were not there.

I fell to the ground,

And gripped the grainy sea,

Where I ask the Creator,

Is my helper?

Even though I can walk,

I may as well be without these legs,

There are no directions in the dark.

I now see in colours,

The colours of life,

The colours of day,

The colours of moods,

I feel their movements,
The aura and air that swirls around them,
Some are still and sweet,
Others sour and thunderous.

This one is a night,
She is a high light,
My lover is like daybreak,
Bringing joy every morning.

I hear what they do not,
And feel those that pass,
I may have no sight but still, I see,
I see better than those with.

My sense of feeling is just as good,
The great object of light that escaped me,
The one that sees,
But does not see itself.

Where could he be?

I . . . miss his arms around me,

And our conversations,

Why punish me further.

My love,

This was not our intention,

This was not what we agreed,

I . . . this is too heavy for me.

My heart,

I ...,

Remember the promises we made,

The words of power we exchanged.

I smile,

But you cannot see the width of my grin,

If only you can see the radiance of my heart,

But still, I revel in your return.

Why all the quietness,

Where are the wilder-beasts?

I cannot hear my people,

Surely I am not in a strange land.

I walk this path daily,

But the landmarks are gone,

Where is the tree of Suiy,

And the rock in Eumkl,

Where is the stone?

That I used to seat,

I cannot hear the birds,

Surely, their choruses are not that faint.

My love,

I still long for you,

I searched high and low,

But still, you hide.

Do you look for me too?

Do you remember me still?

Of course you do,

Oh, how can you forget about me?

Where are you?

They said you were back,

That you had returned from your journey,

I knew you would.

For it was the only light,

That kept me strong,

I want to feel you again,

Trace your face with mine.

Oh, where is he?

After all this time,

Where is he?

Where are you?

The grainy sea has gone silent,

Neither does the high sea announce the rain,

I have waited long for a day like this,

What I'm I to do,

Don't tell me you are looking for me,

On the other side of the Sube,

It will take you forever,

To get from there, to here.

These paths have changed,

A river was not here yesterday,

Am I in a different place?

A different settlement.

My love why are you hiding,

I long for you,

Surely, you have not forgotten about me,

Your girl Jelë.

Well, I will wait until my siblings return,

And we will look for you,

My fear of losing has gone,

Because you are now back.

My guiding light,

My night light,

My high light,

My mirror,

My paradise,

My waterfall of ltoi,

My blue sea of dreams,

My river of patience,

My source of energy,

My very being.

Where are you? . . .

Chapter Sixteen

BLIND

It has been seven days now and still, you have done nothing. Everytime I ask, you keep saying that it is not in your hands.

Where then is the wisdom you demonstrated to me earlier Takunta?

Are you not supposed to the wisest thing living?

Safarai, are you not bestowed with talents beyond talents?

I plea, open your Ball of Wonder, empty it, throw it all on the ground maybe there is something in there that you have overlooked. Maybe you have forgotten that you have something in there that can cure her. Surely you can do it, you can make her see.

Would she have to walk through fire?

Which rare wilder-beast would she have to find?

What part of its body would she need for the sacrifice?

Can I help her build the shrine?

Who will help her?

There must be something we can do. I asked all these questions, but they remained quite, their heads bowed and unable to console me. Answer me, wise ones; do not leave me in this thicket of despair. Surely in all your years, you have cured such a thing before? Surely you know the herbs that we need; surely the chants we need to read are not forgotten by you.

Let us ask the tree, though fallen, I am sure they will still creek with a voice. Let us consult the rocks; shattered but they will still speak.

Where are the flies and the birds of knowledge that carry wisdom on their backs?

Let us catch them, ask them, beg them, and seek them. Surely this is not a new thing to them.

'Is the answer buried in the deep of the deepest?'

'Is it on top of the highest high?'

What of the Book of the Scribes, even the forbidden

scribes?

'Can we not consult these?'

'There must be something we can do.

'What of the trees, the once endowed with walking and seeing, this is the time to reward the gift my ancestors gave them? Even though the land is turned upside down those that were near are now far and things afar must have given up their elusiveness. Surely it will be easier now to reach those things that were once difficult, I am sure not all perished.

'What of the Goddess of the forest, and the Choord bird?'

You said that there is life in everything remember. Well, the hot river still runs and the air still blows. These carry life:

'Am I not correct?'

'Can we not tell them to help, ask for their assistance, advice, anything . . . something?"

'Why, why has the rock stopped hearing, why has the leaf stopped seeing?'

Safarai, you said before that: '...sometimes the things that are living are dead and those that are dead are in the land of reveling' What if this is the case? That all are just at the crossroad.

'Can we bring the land back, can we bring all back, to life?

You said the Sube-mai tree was where the Dynasties wrote their history, story, events. Let us find the fallen mighty giants and consult their ribbed skins. Surely words will come, surely they will let go of their knowledge.

Safarai, speak to the rain, speak to the high light, and the hills and mountains your wives, tell them, beg them to make a return. Tell fire, your passion, tell her to hold off her anger; tell her to appease the fury of the hot flowing river.

'Why are you both silent?'

Give me the Ball of Wonder, let me make her see.

'Which animals bone is this?'

'What bone do I put where?'

'Where do these twigs, shells, and carvings go again?

Show me, show me what to do.

'How do I arrange them?' Tell me what to say to bring her sight back.

'Safarai, Mystery, Takunta, why are you not talking?'

Two things I feared more than death, the first is the blue sea, the second, the dark. The blue sea I can avoid as not to drown; death, that is inevitable, but the dark; surely it is also like death. To me, darkness is death and death is darkness.

'What could be worse than having sight only briefly and the loosing it?'

If a child is born blind at least he is not teased; this is cruelty at its full blossom.

'Why wave the sweet aroma of food to the hungry and then take it from them. '

'Why forbid the thirsty to drink in the rain?'

Imagine the pain she must have felt; imagine the pain she is feeling after all these years; in the damp dark. Surely, we miss that which we have had more that not having those we desire.

We only know day because we know night; we only know life because of its companion, death. Maybe life is merely death delayed, and death, life waiting.

Not having, not knowing, surely these are better than mislaying wisdom, bought with the sweat of labour.

'Who misses life the most I wonder?'

'Is it those still to be born or those that only pay it a brief visit?'

'Perhaps, it is those at the end of their season hoping not to fall accidentally, into a deep sleep. Answer me Takunta, oh Safarai, keep not silent.

The closest experience I have to blindness is in my sleep, here I fear not, for soon, I know I will leave its frightful world, and be alive again. I wonder how often she dreams when she falls asleep.

'How much imagination can you take out of the darkness, when it is your sole dwelling place?'

'How much vision can someone see, when it is no longer an occasion that we look forward to?'

'What if there was no difference between the day and the night, does the day still count?'

Tell me Takunta; oh Safarai, keep silent not now.
Of all the senses in the body, the eye must be the most valued. If I cannot speak but can see, I will be happy to reside in the arms of silence. If I can see but cannot hear, maybe I can use my inner ear and open my inner mind. But darkness I cannot bear.

'How else can we convey the beauty that surrounds us . . . properly?'

'How can we comprehend it?'

It must be difficult to only feel the high light and not see it; to only hear voices and not those that uttered it. Without eyes that see we are dependent, deprived. Lonely will we stand in life for we cannot share in the joy others have.

In the dark, everything becomes smeared with fear, the footsteps, and the touch. Even sound puts on the illusion of a masquerade. Dread becomes the only familiar landscape; vast ahead of us.

In the dark, anything and everything become frightening, surely it is in its grasp that we really appreciate the light. The dark is an empty void, and it's well of despair is never ending.

To see is taken for granted by the seers; we only know the full power of hunger at the absolute absence of food. We only know the full power of the dark when we cannot easily take off its armour. Darkness is difficult, it is unforgiving.

In the dark, we become like wilder-beasts whose dreams only stay in their heads. We grope about the way ahead, only imagining great exploits.

Oh Creator, what can I do, what must I do?

Chapter Seventeen

A S K

Nzé did you ever ask:

Who Takunta was?

Did you question who Safarai is?

If I am to ask you what or who Mystery is, what would your response be?;

In your discussions did you question their intentions or consider fully Safarai marriage to the fire, the rain, even the high light?;

Why was he expelled by the Dynasties and why had the wilder-beasts rejected him as a companion?

Did you not ask why Takunta was in agreement with the wilder-beast to destroy your people? Were you not concerned when he said he wished he could breathe life back into the dead bones of the wilder-beasts that the Dynasties wore around their necks?

Do you know what the Smoke of Truth is?
Do you know who wrote the forbidden scribes?

Cast your mind back, Mystery said that Safarai had polluted the rivers and turned the once lush garden of the East to a barren land - what did you think he meant?

Why were the Dynasty of the North completely destroyed and lost all that they had? Do you think it was fate, decided by the Creator?

Were Safarai and Takunta sent to save you?

Why do you say that the dark and the blackness of the night are evil? Why does it furnish the landscape ahead with terror and put fear in everything?

Well, I will tell you these and much more Nzé.

Chapter Eighteen

CHOSEN

The Tiron-tamada was not your people's fate, neither was it meant that the jaws of the Beasts of the Night were to take life from them. The event was planned and coerced by many individuals but the main protagonist was Takunta.

Takunta was a wilder-beasts. He was the alpha male of the all and had great powers bestowed onto him. However, as he had previously done, as always will be, he was challenged by another male to take over the pride. Takunta had reigned many years without any real contest or challenges, but two young bulls had decided that it was their turn to take over the pride. Takunta not used to having to ward-off two persistent, aggressive attackers lost his reign to the young brothers. However, he was determined to take his reign back.

Wounded and helpless, he was approached by the spirits in the forest that promised to give him back his seat as the leader and give him strength and wisdom to do so, but for a price. He was to write the book of the Forbidden Curses. Thinking it was going to be brief; he agreed and started as directed. How was a wilder-beast going to transcribe words and document you may ask? Well, the spirits chanted for him and over him so that his front hinds became like the arms of the Dynasties.

They made it so that he could speak, hear and converse with the Dynasties and the spirits in the forests. So they started. He documented rituals, incantations, spells, sacrifices, antidotes, and all manners of things. In them: How to turn a Frog into a bird; How to curse a bird so it cannot fly so it could be caught; Making eight legged wilder-beasts. How to make poisons those to put in water, in meat, in the field, in the air in rivers and streams. They taught him how to make things disappear. In it was how to merge a Dynastic with wilder-beasts, or with the fish in the sea. The list went on and the book grew thicker.

One day Takunta realised that he had been writing

the book for over ten years and had forgotten about the pride he was to lead and take back - his main reason for doing the writing in the first place. Frustrated that they did not tell him how long it was going to take, he decided to leave the spirits and their book and go back to take his pride. Even before he left the forest he realised that this was not going to be possible; for they had changed his body and appearance.

His front legs were now like arms like the Dynasties, his head was much smaller, he could not run with force and power like other wilder-beasts. He went back and asked the spirits to change him back but they refused as he had broken the promise they originally made. They said you promised to write the Forbidden scribes which you agreed. You did not ask how long it was going to be for. The answer he thought in his mind was: Eternity.

Now bound to the forest, even the wilder-beasts he wanted to lead flee from him when they see him from a dis-tance. He knew this was how he is going to be for the rest of his life. Now alone, with no book, and the spirits had turned their back on him, he was at a loss as to what to do. But, he was able to remember the some of the scribes he had written, but none that would turn him back to a wilder-beasts that he once was. There was only one thing that would cure him, it resided in the land to the North of the land.

He managed to convince other wilder-beasts, through charms and amulets, that he was attacked by the Dynasties and they had done this to him. He made up a story about how they had caught him, tortured him and wanted to turn him into a breed of half Dynastic and half wilder-beasts. Therefore, he had the most severe hatred for the Dynasties, all of them. He decided to kill and wipe all the Dynasties off the face of the land, starting with the Dynasty of the North.

They, responding under the spell, agree to help him and bring the Dynasties down. It was then they agreed to use the Beasts of the Night, the most powerful and feared beasts in the land to carry out the attacks. However, he did not tell them the real reason for attacking the Dynasty to the North first. Why? Because there laid the secret to his cure, his access to power again. The thing that resided to the North of the land held the key to regaining his youthful and dominance over all the wilder-beasts.

However, to his dismay, after the attack was carried out, he went to and through the dead bodies and carcasses. He searched the abodes and all the tunnels dug. He searched

the hills and rocks and waded through rivers and streams
but could not found the one thing he desired, the one thing
that was the reason for the Tiron-tamada.

Safarai, on his hunt one day, came across the book, in
the middle of the forest, part open. Intrigued by what the
bark-covered object was, as it lay, reflecting the high light.
Walked over, picked it up and started looking through it. Not
knowing, he turned the page back and forth. It was full of
symbols and diagrams he could not understand.

A little while later, a young boy appeared to him and
said:

'Read me a story,'

He looked at the child and asked whether the book belonged to him. The child, unresponsive, said again:

'Read me a story.'

He took the book from Safarai and opened it. Pointing
at a page with symbols and signs he couldn't read, Safarai
commented that he doesn't understand what was written
and scrolled on the book. The boy turns and said:

'I will teach you.

Surprised by the child's response, and thinking to be kind to him, Safarai sat there and repeated after the child.

The child of cause was not an ordinary child. He was the spirit of the forest manifested in the form of the boy. What Safarai did not realised was that he was agreeing to take on the role of the scribe and will do it until whenever it was to be completed. A short time later, reading as directed earlier by the boy, Safarai looked up and the child was gone.

He tried to get up but was held down by the tree he sat on, its branches quickly wiped round and tied him to the tree, pulling him hard against it, strapping his arms and legs so that he could not move. Then appeared what looked like a figure ahead of him, and instructed him as to what to do.

He had been told to go and send strive amongst the Dynasties, to cause havoc, unrest, turmoil amongst all the Dynasties. He journeys to the West and to the East, he went to the South and the North. Seeing that his words were not been fully received and followed, he decided to take drastic steps.

Standing on Mount Sumbiti, he stretched forth his hands to wards the land to the East of the land. Took out the book of the Forbidden scribes and started chanting. He cursed river Rutenoi-pyepe to the East that all that drink from it shall be poisoned. Raising his staff over his head, he pointed it to the East again, and commanded the lush garden to become a desert place. Fire came from his staff and swept through the land. Now he said, hunger will force you to fight and wage war against all your neighbours, being that they feared those of the East already because of their size. Unfortunate for him, only part of the land was consumed by the grainy sea.

Not wanting to give up he retired briefly and consulted the book again. This time the spirits appeared unto him and said what he wanted to do was too power for him. That he needed to attain a higher level of authority to do such a great thing. He decided to proceed. It was there they told him that he could only do such a thing if he gives up half of his life.

Consumed in rage, anger swirled in his eye. With the book in one hand and staff in the other, he said: 'I will do it.' It was then they explained that he had to give part of his life to many of natures elements, like the fire, the rain, the hills etc. In agreeing, he became part of these and they, part of him. In essence, he married them. Now full of power, he went back to the mountain and cursed the land to the East again. This time the grainy sea lifted swirled to his voice and flooded the gardens. This is the reason why the Dynasty of the East spend a quarter of the year underground because of the swirling battling rage of the grainy sea which no one could quench.

Impressed by what his master had achieved, his understudy Yijugukabu wanted the same power. There was only one way to get this - steal the Forbidden scribes book. Safarai woke up from a sleep during the high light one day and saw the book was gone and with it Yijugukabu. He rose up and cursed him saying whenever Yijugukabu ever wanted to use the book, that the opposite of what he wishes for should happen to him. Unaware, Yijugukabu for simply wanting to be the best hunter in the hand was afflicted with the curse and wandered the land laced with the spirit of madness.

Yijugukabu Izaka brought Takunta and Safarai together because after Takunta cured him he explained what had happened to him. This was when Takunta approached Safarai to help him look for the cure that had plagued him all this time.

Safarai also had an interest in the thing which Takunta wanted. The intestines, skin and other parts were to be used to cure his ailments. Following the near fatal attack of the beast and the curses he carried because of the wickedness he had done, the spirits had required this for his atonement. If you look at Safarai close, look again. The thing on his back that looks like a hump is not that at all. That is where he carries the Forbidden scribes. This is the reason why he avoids the forest for they want their belonging back from him. After years of constant torment many sacrifices were required and each time, the requests got graver.

Indeed, as Mystery said, he has sacrificed the forbidden beasts on the grainy sea and the blue sea; used the beaks and claws of the rare bird. In his Ball of Wonder lies one-half of the Choord bird's claw, the other resides in the land of the West. The long feathers you see him wear on his back; hanging over his head to the back of his feet are those of the Choord bird. He had tried to kill it before, as requested of him. Not knowing that not all things can be killed, not all ambitions are fulfilled; not all wishes come to past.

He managed to follow the Choord bird to its resting place hoping to catch it whilst asleep, not knowing that the Choord sleeps not. He crept up the unforgiving mountain *face. Up and through the jagged terrain; crawled through the rock lined ground, and entered. Safarai had followed the one given equivocal protection into its abode, the Cave of Ofjutei.*

At his arrival, he saw nothing but had just shortly watched the Choord enter. Quietly, unwrapping himself in the darkness of the cave. He laid down his staff and put the Ball of Wonder to one side. He took off the ropes used to hold the book up high on his back, swung it under his left arm; the book landed with a thud. He clapped his hand and light shone. Now the glowing colours of the high light filled the dark cave. Turning the mixtures of leaves and barks used to make the book quickly backward and forward. He got to the page he needs. The title read: LIFE FOR LIFE.

As the heading suggested, he wanted to take the life of the most precious creature in the air, second only to the Dynasties. Turning to his Ball of Wonder, gently, he unwrapped it. Taking out his amulets waving it back and forth, he read the scribes. The Choord Bird, perched on the side of the cave looked on. He drew a large circle on the ground, sprinkled the crumbled rocks of Sumbiti inside the circle, whispered a few scribes and the circle was ablaze with fire. Throwing in-

cense, barks of trees of many species in, he began to chant the words: Choord..., Choord..., Choord, over and over again.

Still, the Choord looked on unmoved. After almost a day of chanting with no response, frustrated and choking in the smoke-filled cave; he quickly gathered all his possessions. With the book on his back, he hobbled swiftly out of Ofjutei.

Not wanting to leave empty handed, he gathered a few feathers laying around Mount Sumbiti, stitched them together, soaked them in blood and made them look like it was one feather. He left. He was now telling the Dynasties that the feathers belonged to the Choord, acquired after a long bitter battle. Deceiving them, he said that this was where his supernatural power laid - with the book hidden out of sight, roped to his body, under his cloak, covered with make-shift Choord bird's feathers.

This indeed must be a powerful man they gasped, having fought the Choord and survived. It was this that he used to make people listened to him, spewing his mind-changing, charm-coated words, as he turned one Dynasty against another. He encouraged the Dynasties to divide the land and have boundaries to each settlement. He told the strong powerful people to dwell in the East, the beautiful, his favourites, to reside to the West. The Dynasty of the South, he said, were now to be seen as the enemy. Favoured by the Creator he said, they sit in the high sea, begging for the Creator to favour them more. He divided the Dynasties.

His meal of wickedness he baked and fed to the Dynasties and the wilder-beasts. They consumed it perilously. It became the water they drank; the air they breathed. Later, when all discovered his intention and his curses broke; they all banished him from their settlement. However, the seed he planted in the Dynasties now ran in their blood streams; strive raged continuously with no real cause.

The fruits of his work engulfed the Dynasty of the West and they eat, they in-turn fed it to the Dynasty of the East. Although the spell over them was broken they had unfortunate wrote it into their laws; wickedness coloured their future outlook.

Nzé, you mentioned that at the outset, following the Tiron-tamada, you had fruits and berry to eat in plenty, you took vegetable and meat as and when you which. Takunta and Safarai with Yijugukabu, all made a pack. Knowing the Chosen was out in the land somewhere and had escaped their plan, they now look to turn the lush, fertile land into vast wilderness.

The Chosen, they said, will be starved out of hiding. They inflicted the land, poisoned rivers and cursed the fields to give the Chosen hunger and strive. The sole purpose: TO FIND THE CHOSEN ONE FROM THE DYNASTY OF THE NORTH, NZÉ.

Takunta needed your still beating heart for his ritual; Safarai, your running rare blood for his atonement. They made a pact that whoever found you first must deliver you Safarai. After your encounter with Takunta, he followed you and relayed information to Safarai as to your whereabouts.

Takunta is indeed wise but used it in the wrong way. However, he is not the wisest thing in the land of Nza, how could he be, he is but a wilder-beast, a deformed one at that.

Takunta's story about the three seas was just to entertain you; to gain your trust so that you accept them.

'Do you think that the Creator needed a tree, a Sube-

mai tree to make his decision stand?'

The tree indeed is the tallest in the land. The Dynasties wanted to attach other meanings to it, so they did. They made their abode atop of it saying they wanted to be closer to the Creator. Surely, they of all the Dynasties know that the Creator is everywhere. That he is not high up there, far off, at a long distance; rather, that he resided in each and everyone of them.

The high sea, the blue sea, and the grainy sea had always been separated; it was how the Creator made them. They use the circumstances they created - that his, you were a young orphan, lost in the wilderness to convince you, knowing the only person you can console for redirection was your mind.

You were right to disagree with Takunta. Rocks are not alive; neither can a tree walk, nor is their branches befitted with eyes. Consider this.

'When the wind blows a dried leaf that has fallen on the ground, does that mean the leaf is alive?'

Also, 'why is it that of all the creatures that can move

and walk, it is only the tree that chose to stand still, all the time?'

'Is it because it is shy of on-lookers and passer by?' Aware that you were not convinced, he changed the story to Safarai having six wives.

'Did you stop to consider how a person can be married to fire, or the rain or the high light for that matter?'

All these were done to make themselves wise in your eyes. To keep you away from the real reason they wanted to gain your trust – to sacrifice you: take your still beating heart and drink your still-warm blood.

Your eyes were opened as Safarai came and approached you.

'Did you know what he was doing as he staggered to the left and to the right?'

As the Forbidden scribes commanded, he was honouring the spirits of the forest in three ways when he found you. This act was to symbolise the existence and union of all living things.

Firstly, by staggering, he was giving honour to the wilder-beasts of the field; mimicking the motions of the mammals in the blue sea.

Secondly, when he bowed his head and turned around with his arms spread, he was making adoration to the spirits of the air; the birds of the high sea.

Thirdly, he offered himself to complete the thread of life.

All these acts were offered up as burnt offerings, hence the fire. When he sat, he had the Forbidden scribes opened in front of him; you could not see it as he hid it in the Ball of Wonder.

When he said that he saw the colour of your eyes red like blood and that you whispered something but he did not hear it. This indeed was true, your spirit was confirming to the ones he evoked that your life was sacred, as the Chosen, that success was not going to be theirs.

Safarai, like other Dynasties he encouraged to keep of-fering sacrifices forgot something. That slaughtering beasts and making sacrifices is not what is required or what makes their offerings acceptable, rather, it is the belief and the hu-

mility before their acts of cruelty.

Mystery commented and said that Safarai 'dined with the damned'. This is also true. In following Safarai's sacrifice, all that he offers on the shrine is consumed raw by him and the spirits that the offerings were made for. They all gather together and consume the filth food. Using their mouth only, they knock heads aggressively, pulling the intestines, skins, bladder of the innocent preys from each other's mouths. Blood splashes on their faces, as the colour of life flushes and foams between their teeth.

The Smoke of Truth is anything but the truth. Rather a foul concoction of abominable stench, worse than a rotten corpse. It is what he uses to en-trance his victims, a channel to climb into their soul. After ransacking their gifts, talents, and blessings; he replaces them with curses and premature death. Only the Creator can save. Fake seers are but these, they seek not the Spirit of truth.

The hunger and distress you experience in the wilderness was indeed to keep alive, to keep you moving, away and out of their reach. They too went through the same thing you did. You were kept safe; they were punished for the wickedness. Their judgement will soon come.

Did they not all see the transformation of the Rameta bird? The Creator lifted him up for all to see, surely, they remembered the day time stood still for him?

'Can they not remember; the day he was made-anew?'

'How many wilder-beats did the Rameta bird offered before his voice was heard?

'How many rivers did he curse?

'Which part of the land did he destroy to exchange for his deliverance?'

'Which repulsive incense did he burn, before been crowned the king of the air?'

'Before his feathers grew anew, and the warts dropped off his face; before his eyes were cleaned and legs grew equal, whose blood was he required to taste?'

They all witnessed it. Ask them.

'Who noticed his blood-stained beak and the droplets

of life running down his chest before been revived?'

Recall the story Nzé. Did your good father make mentioned that a life of a wilder-beast was needed or that a male in his prime from the Dynasty of the East was required before he was made better?

Though capable, they rather not wait with patience, minor pains, they seek quick solutions; none, it seems are willing to mature with trials. Truth is given to the Dynasties yet they seek folly; wisdom seeks to be their ally, yet they hunger after death. The Creator made all on the grainy sea, the high sea, and the blue sea; all this he gave to them in plenty. From its North point to the furthest point in the South, all were made for their advantage; from the highest point of the land to the sole of the Abyss of Alvi, it was all for their existence and enjoyment.

'Did you not ask the Dynasty of the South why they made their settlement at the flooding nostrils of the land?'

They knew of the flood before settling, dangling like an abandoned fruit, clinging to the necks of the Sube-mai.

Similarly, the Dynasty of the West knew of the temper of the hot running river that blesses the face of Mount Sumbiti. They chose to live in the cold hills of Mount Bilaguro because of the treasures she hides in her core; they have attached importance to the crystal rock of many colours in the belly of the Hills of Stalia. River Rutenoi-pyepe and the Abyss of Alvi are no mystery to Creator. All were created for a purpose.

The Dynasties, my most beloved, now live within the boundary of their self-created fate. The birds of the high sea and the mammals of the blue sea limit themselves not as them. Suffocating in their self-made caves, they question why the hot river runs; in their folly, they blame the Great Plain's floods.

'Nzé, why do you see the dark and the black of the night as panic?'

'Do you not know that the night is just as important as the day? Or was it just created as a barrier to life?

'Why have you coloured the great entity with thought of fear?'

'Do you not know that the night, just like the day, har-

bours creativity and births ideas? Many creativity, ideas, and inventions are indeed given in the dark sight of light.

Jelë is dear to the Creator. You were made to be friends from birth. You were both born on the same day and she was to be your friend, your companion, your helper, but look what has happened to her. Maybe, this is what has coloured your outlook about the dark. You, imagining that she must be in constant fear, that her imaginations are all nightmares. You seem to have concluded that maybe all she sees, like you, is the daily dose of despair.

Fear not, only one word is needed from the Creator and all will be well.

Chapter Nineteen

LIGHT

Look Nzé.

Look again.

'Can you see her?'

Gelë – Gira ploirante,

Gelë - is alive

Yes, she can also see.

The Creator issued a decree,

Sent a word and she was cured.

EPHPHATHA, THE VOICE said.

THE END

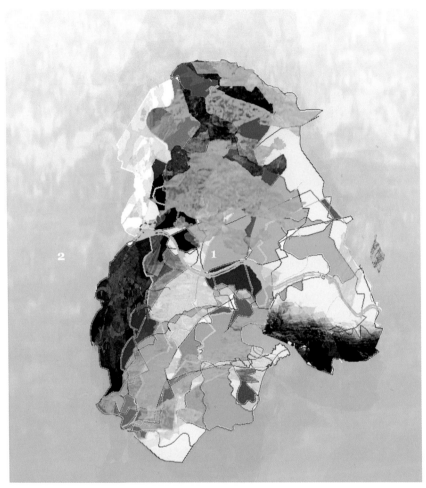

MAP OF NZA

LEGEND:

1) LAND OF NZA
2) THE BLUE SEA

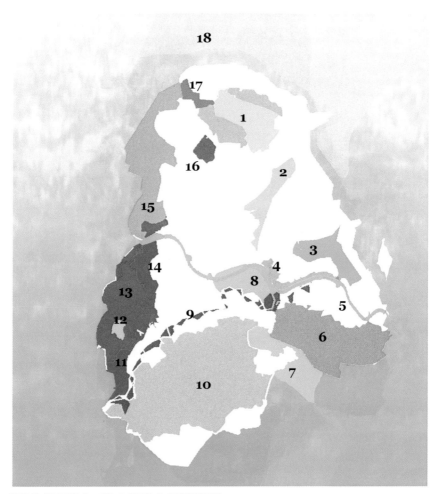

MAP OF NZA - PLACES & EVENTS

LEGEND:

1) EVENT OF *TIRON-TAMADA*
2) LAKE *ISKOYI*
3) OASIS OF THE EAST
4) WILDER-BEASTS MIGRATION/CROSSING
5) RIVER *RUTENOI-PYEPE*
6) HILLS OF *SANDOSA*
7) MOUTH OF *INCABIH*
8) VALLEY OF *ISALAMATA*
9) *SUBE-MAI* TREES

10) THE GREAT PLAINS
11) HILLS OF *STALIA*
12) RAMETA BIRD'S RENEWAL
13) FLOWING HOT RIVER
14) MOUNT *SUMBITI*
15) MOUNT *BILA-GURO*
16) ROCKS OF *UZELETO*
17) WATERFALL OF *ITOI*
18) THE ABYSS OF *ALVI*

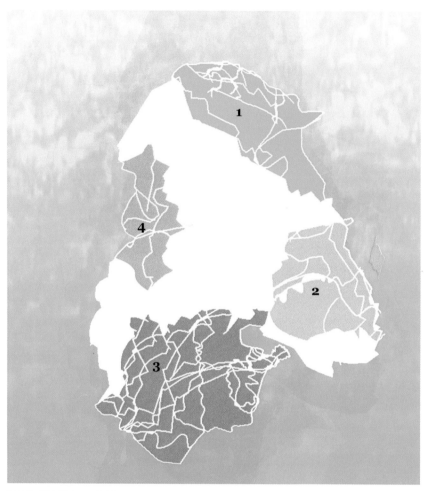

MAP OF NZA - SETTLEMENTS

LEGEND:

1) TRIBE OF THE NORTH
2) TRIBE OF THE EAST
3) TRIBE OF THE SOUTH
4) TRIBE OF THE WEST

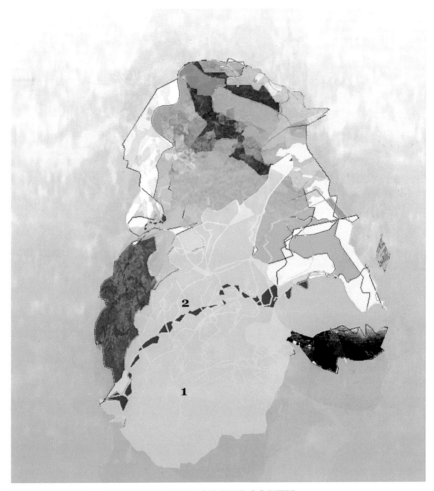

MAP OF NZA - GREAT FLOOD OF THE SOUTH

LEGEND:

1) THE GREAT FLOOD
2) *SUBE-MAI* TREES

MAP OF NZA - DESERT/FAMINE

LEGEND:

1) FAMINE TO NORTH, EAST & WEST
2) LUSH LANDSCAPE TO THE SOUTH

MAP OF NZA - DESERT/FAMINE PERCEIVED BY NZÉ

LEGEND:

1) HIGHEST POINTS ON THE LAND (AS PERCEIVED BY NZÉ)

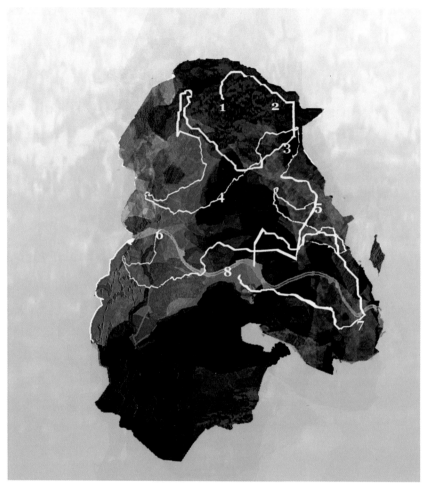

MAP OF NZA - NZÉ'S JOURNEY IN THE WILDERNESS

LEGEND:

1) START OF JOURNEY, EVENT AT *TIRON-TAMADA*
2) VOICE OF NZÉ'S MOTHER (1)
3) THE SINGLE RULE VISION
4) VISION OF THE GOLDEN GOBLET NEAR LAKE *ISKOYI*
5) MEETING WITH TAKUNTA
6) JOURNEY ALONG RIVER *RUTENOI-PYEPE*
7) VOICE OF NZÉ'S MOTHER (2)
8) END OF JOURNEY - VALLEY OF *ISALAMATA*

MAP OF NZA - *SUBE-MAI* **TREES**

LEGEND:

1) *SUBE-MAI* TREES

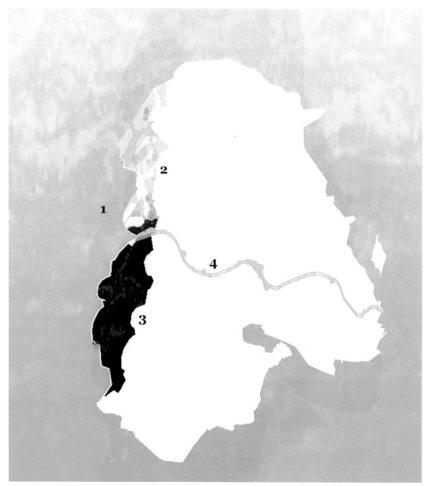

MAP OF NZA - ALLEGORY OF KING'S FACE

LEGEND:

1) PROFILE OF KING'S 'FACE'
2) ICE ON HIS EYES (MOUNT *GILA-BURO*)
3) 'FIRE IN HIS BREATH' (MOUNT *SUMBITI*)
4) 'WORDS BRING LIFE' (RIVER *RUTENOI-PYEPE*)

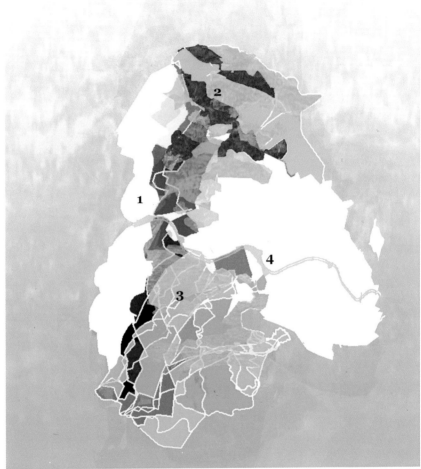

MAP OF NZA - ALLEGORY OF QUEEN'S FACE

LEGEND:

1) PROFILE OF QUEEN'S 'FACE' (RIDGE ALONG MOUNT *GILA-GURO*)
2) OUTLINE OF QUEEN'S 'CROWN' (LAND TO THE NORTH)
3) OUTLINE OF QUEEN'S 'JEWELERY' (LAND TO THE SOUTH)
4) 'WORDS BRING LIFE' (RIVER *RUTENOI-PYEPE*)

MAP OF NZA - ALLEGORY OF PRINCE'S FACE

LEGEND:

1) PROFILE OF PRINCE'S 'FACE' (LAND TO THE NORTH)
2) PRINCE'S WATERY 'EYES' (LAKE *ISKOYI*)

MAP OF NZA - ALLEGORY OF PRINCESS'S FACE

LEGEND:

1) PROFILE OF PRINCESS'S 'FACE' (LAND TO THE EAST)
2) OUTLINE OF HER 'GREEN EYES' (OASIS OF THE EAST)
3) OUTLINE OF HER 'TREASURED PEARLS' (*SUBE-MAI* TREES)

Blank page

Blank page